*He'd felt it. No doubt she'd seen it.* **Need.**

Pure. Primal. Standing right there at the bathroom door. The idea of her taking off her clothes and stepping into the shower had abruptly consumed him. The desire to climb into that shower with her had been fierce.

Not once in years had he felt the compulsion for sex. Nor had he been attracted to any woman with whom he'd worked or encountered outside work. He'd assumed that component of his life was over. The part of his brain that reasoned using his formal training understood that it would take time for him to get over the tragic loss of his wife, physically and emotionally.

But his less rational side had opted not to allow that kind of pain again. The only way to avoid it was to avoid contact with another human on that level.

He'd been completely successful until now…until Sande Williams.

# CAST OF CHARACTERS

**Patrick O'Brien** – He's working his first field assignment, but he has trust issues that may get in the way.

**Sande Williams** – She has no idea who she is or where she came from. The only thing she knows for sure is that anyone who might be able to help her keeps ending up dead.

**Windy Millwood** – Former marine captain, Windy is one of the Colby Agency's best investigators.

**Victoria Colby-Camp** – The head of the Colby Agency.

**Lucas Camp** – A CIA legend and the man who owns Victoria's heart.

**Nancy Childers** – A former co-worker of Sande's. Or is she?

**Alma Spears** – She claims to know all about Sande.

**Detective Lyons** – The homicide detective following the bodies piling up in Sande's wake.

**Detective Cates** – Lyons's partner who has been left out of the loop.

**Special Agent Wheeler** – An enigma. Does he really exist or is he a part of Sande's make-believe world?

**Special Agent-in-Charge Young** – Head of Chicago's FBI field office.

**Simon Ruhl and Ian Michaels** – Victoria's second-in-command.

**Angela Tapley** – Is she really working with the FBI? Or is she also make-believe?

# Identity Unknown
# DEBRA WEBB

MILLS & BOON
Pure reading pleasure™

*All the characters in this book have no existence outside the
imagination of the author, and have no relation whatsoever to anyone
bearing the same name or names. They are not even distantly inspired
by any individual known or unknown to the author, and all the
incidents are pure invention.*

*First published in Great Britain 2009
by Harlequin Mills & Boon Limited,
Eton House, 18-24 Paradise Road, Richmond, Surrey TW9 1SR*

© Debra Webb 2008

*ISBN: 978 0 263 87296 5*

46-0609

*Harlequin Mills & Boon policy is to use papers that are
natural, renewable and recyclable products and made from
wood grown in sustainable forests. The logging and
manufacturing processes conform to the legal environmental
regulations of the country of origin.*

*Printed and bound in Spain
by Litografia Rosés S.A., Barcelona*

## *ABOUT THE AUTHOR*

Debra Webb was born in Scottsboro, Alabama, to parents who taught her that anything is possible if you want it badly enough. She began writing at the age of nine. Eventually, she met and married the man of her dreams, and tried some other occupations, including selling vacuum cleaners, working in a factory, a daycare centre, a hospital and a department store. When her husband joined the military, they moved to Berlin, Germany, and Debra became a secretary in the commanding general's office. By 1985 they were back in the States, and finally moved to Tennessee, to a small town where everyone knows everyone else. With the support of her husband and two beautiful daughters, Debra took up writing again, looking to mystery and movies for inspiration. In 1998, her dream of writing came true. You can write to Debra with your comments at PO Box 64, Huntland, Tennessee 37345, USA or visit her website at http://www.debrawebb.com to find out exciting news about her next book.

Sometimes we search high and low and can't seem to figure out who we are anymore or what we want. Whether it's a new phase in our lives or just a rough patch, sometimes we question ourselves and our destiny. This book is dedicated to the two women who keep me grounded. They never lose faith in me and never let me forget who I am, what I want and where I'm going in this life. To Donna Boyd and Vicki Hinze. I love you both. Life would be damned hard without you.

# *Chapter One*

She shivered.

Goose bumps rushed over her flesh. God, she was so cold. She hugged the sheet more closely, then wrinkled her nose. Why was the sheet covering her face?

Her eyes opened.

The sheet was over her face!

She snatched it away. Gasped for air, as if the cotton were plastic, and had deprived her of much needed oxygen...

Okay, she was okay.

A frown furrowed her forehead. Where was she?

A hall or corridor. Glaring fluorescent lights hummed overhead. A nasty smell lingered in the air. Something pungent and unfamiliar.

She sat up and blinked, looked around and blinked

again. Dingy white walls…long corridor. A white sheet draped her nude body.

Where were her clothes?

She stared at her breasts…at her flat belly.

What the'…?

A gurney. She was sitting on a gurney. Like in a hospital.

Had she been in an accident?

She looked at her arms and hands, touched her face, ran her fingers through her hair… She didn't feel different. She wasn't in pain. There were no lumps or bumps. No wet sticky spots.

*Where the hell was she?*

She looked around again. Then she saw the door directly across from where her gurney stood.

A plaque on the door marked it as… She squinted. It was…the *morgue*.

Her heart missed a beat.

The morgue?

She stared down at herself once more. No blood. No bruises.

She jerked free of the sheet, stumbled off the gurney and staggered as if she hadn't stood in a long time. Her legs felt weak and rubbery.

What was wrong with her?

Voices. Someone was coming.

She snatched the sheet from the gurney and wrapped it around her naked body. She had to hide.

If they found her… Her mind couldn't grasp the concept of why the unfamiliar voices terrified her, but instinct warned that she should be afraid.

She had to run!

She half stumbled, half fell down the corridor, grabbed the knob of the first door she encountered and yanked it open.

Janitor's closet.

She threw herself inside, closed the door soundlessly and struggled to catch her breath.

*Just breathe. Deep breaths. Slow…steady.*

*You're okay.* You're *okay.*

The stench of cleansers and damp mops assaulted her nostrils. She ignored it. She had to think!

What had happened to her?

Why would she be on a gurney in front of a door marked Morgue?

She wasn't dead.

Was she?

She took a step back from the door and stared down at her foot. A white tag was attached to her big toe.

Panic closed her throat.

*Don't panic.*

She crouched down and reached with trembling hands to remove the tag. Slowly straightening once more, she read the information written there. Sande Williams. Female. Twenty-eight years old. Sixty-four inches tall. One hundred ten pounds.

Why didn't the name ring a bell?

There was no address or telephone number.

What did this mean?

She started to shake, and found she had to brace herself against the closed door in order to remain vertical.

What was wrong with her?

Could she be dead and not know it?

No, that wasn't possible.

As if to deny her assertion, she touched her wrist and counted the beats.

She had a pulse.

She pressed her palm against the center of her chest to feel the frantic pounding there.

She had a heartbeat.

She was alive.

But why didn't she remember how she got here? Was she sick? What had happened to cause her to be in this place? There had to be something wrong with her.

Why didn't the name on the tag *feel* like her name?

Sande Williams.

Fear snaked around her chest and squeezed, sending panic searing through her veins.

She couldn't find any answers in this janitor's closet.

She had to get out of here.

Had to find help.

But what if *they* wouldn't let her go?

Didn't they institutionalize people who couldn't remember their names? Who woke up wearing toe tags for no apparent reason?

*Breathe again. Deep. Hold it. Release.*

*Calm down. Just calm down.*

She needed help.

She had to move.

Slowly, her palms sweating with the fear mounting inside her, she opened the door a crack. She peeked into the corridor. Still deserted. Still quiet.

Someone had taken off her clothes and placed her on that gurney, had put a toe tag on her. Someone thought she was dead.

How was that possible?

Hadn't she seen a movie like that once?

*Think!*

She had to get out of here.

There was something wrong with this place. People who had heartbeats weren't sent to the morgue. There had to be a mistake.

She couldn't stay here.

She ran. Holding the sheet tightly around her, the toe tag clutched in one hand, she ran as fast as she could to escape.

*Don't take the elevator*.

She would be trapped there.

*Take the stairs*.

Up was the only option. She rushed up the steps two at a time. Reached the first floor and burst out of the stairwell.

The lobby.

A massive lobby with a bubbling fountain and towering green plants. People…lots of people.

They stopped and stared at her.

The sheet.

She was naked save for the sheet. Naked and barefoot. What must they think?

A woman wearing a white uniform approached her.

"Ma'am, are you all right?"

The cap, the badge…a nurse.

Nurses helped people…but this one worked *here*.

"I…I'm fine," she insisted. She had to get out of here. The way the nurse looked at her…she was concerned and *suspicious*.

She would call those people who had done this to her.

Still clutching the toe tag, she ran. She couldn't risk having the nurse touch her and tell her she needed to go back to that gurney and lie down because she was dead.

She couldn't be dead.

She was running, escaping the hospital.

Voices shouted behind her, but she just ran faster.

She was alive. She didn't care what anyone said.

As she burst out onto the sidewalk, the wind slapped her in the face. The icy sting made her quivering lips stretch into a wobbly smile. The cold of the concrete beneath her feet reinforced the conclusion.

Yes, she was alive.

Two men dressed in dark uniforms rushed from the same door she had exited and headed toward her. They shouted for her to stop.

She ran—darted between the moving cars as horns blared. She ignored them.

She had to hurry, had to run faster.

If they caught her…it would be bad. She didn't know why, but she sensed that her life depended upon her getting away from this place.

So she didn't stop. Not for the cars. Not for the shouts behind her.

Not for anything.

SHE COULDN'T RUN anymore.

She had to stop.

Cutting to the right, she stumbled to a standstill in an alley. Sande leaned against the brick wall.

Should she call herself Sande?

She thought of the toe tag clutched in her right hand. Maybe.

The alley was deserted, as far as she could tell. She peered toward the end, with its pockets of darkness. Nothing moved. There was no sound, other than the street noises that filtered past the cars parked along the curb and the trees lining the sidewalk.

A Dumpster accompanied by a pile of boxes sat a few yards away. She could hide there for a little while...until she figured out what to do next. Until she wasn't so tired anymore.

Was there someone to call? Would Sande Williams be listed with directory assistance? If she had an address she could start there.

According to the newspapers she'd seen in the newsstands she'd run past, she was in Chicago. If Chicago was home, wouldn't some emotion or memory stir? Shouldn't she feel a connection?

Shouldn't she feel something?

Other than tired. She needed to sit down. Her feet were freezing. Her hands were cold. She shuddered. Her whole body was chilled.

The date on the newspaper had said October 29. Made sense, she supposed, that the temperature outside was cold. It was almost November. Thanksgiving was in November. Snow sometimes came in November. It was supposed to be cold.

How could she remember all those everyday details and not know the first thing about herself? Not her name, her age, her address.

Nothing.

Sande pushed away from the wall. The towering brick buildings on either side of the alley kept the sun at bay. The shadows deepened the farther into the alley she ventured.

She could climb into one of those larger boxes and curl up in a ball to stay warm. That would help. Maybe she'd even put one on top to create a sort of shelter the way homeless people did.

Anticipation trickled inside her.

Was she homeless? A kind of sadness filtered through her. Did Sande Williams have anyplace to go? Any family? Friends? Or was she completely alone?

She couldn't worry about that right now. Staying warm took priority. Survival had to come first.

She reached for a box. It was just what she needed.

"Hey! That's my box!"

Sande jerked her hand away. Lurched back a couple of steps. "I'm…I'm sorry."

The stringy-haired lady who had scolded her stepped from the shadows beyond the pile of cardboard boxes. Her heavy coat made her look like an Eskimo. "I don't mind sharing," the Eskimo woman said as she swiped her hands against the ragged jeans she wore. "But you should always ask first."

Sande nodded. "Sorry." She hadn't meant to invade anyone else's territory. She was just so tired. Cold and lost. And she was scared. Terrified.

The woman's eyes narrowed as she assessed Sande from forehead to feet. "Where's your clothes, girl?"

Good question. Wearing a white bedsheet certainly didn't count. "I'm not sure what happened." Might as well tell the truth. "I woke up like this."

The woman pursed her lips thoughtfully. She didn't appear that old, just looked a little haphazard and world-weary. Her jeans and coat were old, worn-out.

"I probably got something you could wear."

Sande almost refused her generosity. Clearly, the woman had very little in the way of assets. Sande hated to take anything from her. But at the moment, she was pretty much desperate. Beyond desperate, actually.

Why couldn't she remember anything?

"I'd appreciate that," she said, thankful for the assistance.

The woman motioned with her right arm. "Come on."

She dug her way through the piles of boxes until she reached what might have been the center. Sande realized then that the boxes were stacked in such a way that they created a refuge.

She followed the woman into the cardboard sanctuary. "What's your name?" her new friend asked.

The toe tag clutched in Sande's hand came immediately to mind. Though she hesitated before giving that answer, nothing else occurred to her. "Sande Williams."

"I'm Madge," the older woman said, "but you don't look like a Sande to me."

Sande didn't know what to say to that statement. The name didn't set off even a flicker of recognition within her. And other than her height and weight, she didn't know anything about how she looked. Fear surged inside her once more. How could she not know her own hair color? Or eye color?

She grasped a strand of her hair and pulled it in front of her face. Blond. She had blond hair.

"You from out of town?"

Sande shook off the disturbing questions churning in her brain and nodded, then, with resignation, wagged her head. "I really don't know."

Equal parts suspicion and sympathy stirred in the woman's eyes. "Something wrong with you, girl?"

"Maybe." Sande shrugged. "I'm not certain. I woke up in a—" she cleared her throat "—in a hospital." She swallowed hard. "Dressed like this."

"You don't know how you got there?"

Another shake of her head answered that question.

Madge's eyes narrowed with increasing suspicion. "You ain't got no strange disease, do you?"

Sande bit her bottom lip. She hadn't thought of that. The possibility took her anxiety to a whole new level. "I don't think so."

"Well." Madge considered the situation a moment. "I tell you what." She stooped down and dug through a large plastic shopping bag. The colorful words printed on the bag were partially worn off, as if its owner had lugged it around for quite some time. "You get these clothes on—" Madge offered Sande the items she had retrieved "—and we'll go down to the church and have us some lunch. There's a man who serves there on Thursdays who might be able to help you out."

Did that mean today was Thursday? Didn't really matter. Sande hastily tugged on the clothes. She didn't care what they were or their condition, or even how they fit, as long as they covered her body and protected her from the cold that had settled deep into her bones.

The memory of those men chasing after her back at the hospital reignited her fear, which had lessened a fraction.

"Who is this man?" she asked, a little hesitant to speak to a stranger, considering recent circumstances. Whatever instincts she possessed were screaming at her to use extreme caution.

"His name is Lucas Camp." Madge scrounged around in the bag once more until she came up with a pair of beat-up sneakers. "His wife runs some fancy private investigation agency." She made a humming sound as she mulled over what she wanted to say next. "The Colby Agency."

*Colby Agency?*

Didn't ring any bells for Sande.

"Yep." Madge fished a tattered jacket from her stockpile of personal goods. "They say the Colby Agency is the best of its kind. I bet you they'll be able to figure out just what happened to you and where you come from. Seems like the best plan."

Sande sure hoped so.

She couldn't remember her name or where she lived…but she had a feeling. A very bad feeling that if she didn't get help, something terrible was going to happen…

To her.

# *Chapter Two*

Patrick O'Brien.

Dr. Patrick O'Brien.

No. Not anymore.

Patrick had given up his practice as a psychologist more than two years ago.

He wasn't going back there.

Not ever.

Patrick surveyed his office. He liked working for the Colby Agency. Profiling clients and the subjects associated with cases had proved to be interesting work. The pay was outstanding and the benefits unmatched.

His work kept him busy. He didn't have to think about the past…

Then what the hell was wrong with him today? He couldn't keep his mind on the task in front of him. He felt restless. Out of sorts.

He knew the reason. Pretending wouldn't make it otherwise.

It was the anniversary of his wife's death. Three years ago today she had left their Oak Park home for a day of shopping with friends, but had never made it to the mall. Never even made it across town. A carjacking had left her dead on the street.

And that had only been the beginning of his life's unraveling.

Patrick pushed away the memories, the images that instantly flooded his mind. He couldn't live in the past, couldn't keep looking back. Forcing his focus forward was the only way to survive.

Despite his determination not to dwell on the worst of his history, his thoughts appeared to have a will of their own. For the first few weeks after his wife's murder he'd asked himself why it couldn't have been him. Why her? An angel as surely as he lived and breathed. His angel. That was what she had been.

Or so he had thought. Slowly but surely, as the investigation into her death had played out, he had learned that he'd never really known his wife at all. She had led a double life. Beautiful, devoted wife to him, to all appearances; obsessive-compulsive adulteress when no one was watching.

That old familiar knot formed in his gut. How could he have studied and worked to heal the human mind when he hadn't recognized for a moment that his own wife was a habitual liar and cheater? Not once had he suspected her extramarital activities, and yet there had been dozens of men during their five-year marriage. The wife of one had hired a thug to kill the woman who had lured her husband into temptation.

Nothing Patrick did or felt could change the facts. He couldn't let those painful memories distract him from the present and drag him back into that pit of agony and depression he had slowly risen from two years ago. Wallowing in self-pity and doubt would accomplish nothing, then or now.

He had started over. He had a life here at the Colby Agency. Patrick liked his work. For the most part he kept to himself after hours. No family ties, no social obligations. He didn't need anything else. Nor anyone else.

He trusted no one outside his colleagues at the agency. Even that fledgling bond was strictly in the professional sense. His personal life would remain his alone. If he didn't venture into that trust territory, he wouldn't have to worry about being deceived.

The intercom on his desk buzzed, dragging him from the painful past. Mildred Ballard's voice followed. "Patrick, could you come to Victoria's office? She has a new case she'd like to discuss with you."

"Thank you, Mildred, I'll be right there."

Work was the one thing he depended on now. He could trust his work. It never let him down.

The stroll to Victoria's office was uninterrupted. Most of the investigators on staff were engrossed in cases, with no time for idle chatter. Admittedly, the entire staff operated more like a large family, but that atmosphere of camaraderie never got in the way of solving any case. Meeting or exceeding the client's needs and expectations was paramount to Victoria Colby-Camp.

That was another thing he liked about the agency; no corners were cut, no underhanded business tactics were used. Top-notch investigative work was the order of the day. Patrick was surrounded by the best of the best in the field of private investigations. The Colby Agency's reputation was unparalleled. No one lied. No one cheated.

"She's waiting for you," Mildred said as Patrick approached.

Mildred Ballard had been with Victoria for two decades. Through thick and thin, both would say. As the personal assistant to the woman in charge, Mildred ran a tight ship. She missed nothing and kept everyone in line. Mildred was outranked only by Ian Michaels and Simon Ruhl, Victoria's seconds in command.

Patrick nodded in acknowledgment of Mildred's

broad smile and entered the private office of Victoria Colby-Camp. Lucas Camp, Victoria's husband, rose from one of the chairs flanking the massive desk as Patrick crossed the room.

"Victoria." Patrick looked from his boss to the man whose very presence still intimidated most, even him at times. "Lucas." He extended his hand. "How was your trip?"

Lucas shook Patrick's hand with the same confidence his bearing conveyed, despite the ever-present cane that assisted his less-than-perfect stride. "I accomplished my mission."

And that was all he would be getting from the mysterious Lucas Camp. The man was a CIA legend, though his activities had been and still were cloaked in secrecy. Retirement had done little to slow him. He still worked in an advisory capacity for the government and spent every possible moment with his wife—the woman he had waited twenty years to call his own.

That Lucas Camp was present for this meeting carried a great deal of significance. Patrick was definitely intrigued.

"I wouldn't have expected anything less," he stated as both he and Lucas settled into the comfortable wingback chairs.

"Here's Windy," Victoria announced. "Now we can get started."

Patrick glanced toward the door as Windy Millwood entered the room. He frowned momentarily, but he almost immediately schooled his expression. He was, after all, merely a profiler. He should have anticipated there would be an investigator sitting in. Disappointment niggled, but he pushed it away. When Victoria thought he was ready to get in the field and take on a case, she would say as much. She wasn't one to mince words, nor was she indecisive.

"Sorry I'm late," Windy said. "I was waiting for a fax." Paper in hand, the tall brunette strode to the chair on the other side of Lucas and settled into it. The formal bearing of her military days had carried over to her civilian career.

Male investigators outnumbered females five to one at the Colby Agency, but not one, male or female, was more prepared and well trained than former Marine Captain Windy Millwood.

"Now that we're all here," Victoria began, "let's bring Patrick up to speed."

Lucas began. "Yesterday afternoon one of the regulars at the soup kitchen brought in a sort of Jane Doe."

"Sort of?" Patrick inquired.

Lucas appeared to consider for a moment how to respond, before continuing. "She had a name, but no recall of who she was or where she came from."

As Lucas explained the circumstances of the client's only memories, Patrick found himself increasingly intrigued. He had to confess that waking up covered by a sheet and lying on a gurney outside a morgue door was not an everyday occurrence.

"Her driver's license is a match. Social security number, too," Windy confirmed as she passed the page to Lucas. "But that's where it ends."

Lucas handed the fax to Patrick. "What about the address on the license?"

As Windy explained that the residence recorded on the license was occupied by and belonged to someone else, Patrick considered the blond woman in the DMV photo. Sande Williams. Young. Twenty-eight, according to the birth date shown. Blue eyes. Petite in size.

"Did you visit the residence?" Patrick looked at Windy. "Perhaps Ms. Williams is a friend or relative of the occupant."

"I thought we'd go together," Windy suggested.

"Patrick," Victoria interjected, drawing his attention to her, "you'll be working this case with Windy. Considering the client's apparent amnesia, I felt you would be an asset on this one. I've been waiting for the right opportunity to get you into the field. I believe this is the perfect case."

Anticipation fired in every neuron. "I agree." Patrick had been awaiting this opportunity as well.

That the client had special needs falling within the scope of his former profession was definitely a bonus.

"It might not be a bad idea to take Ms. Williams along on your visit to the residence," Lucas suggested. That he made the statement to him rather than Windy surprised Patrick, since she was unquestionably senior. "If the client has ever lived at that address the encounter could trigger repressed memories."

No doubt, but there could also be hazards related to such a bold move. "With all due respect, Lucas, I'd like to interview the client before taking that step. Just as a precaution."

"Of course," the older man replied. "The mind is your specialty."

"The two of you can get started," Victoria recommended, "and the research team will continue to dig for information on Ms. Williams."

"I'll have a colleague of mine check under a few rocks to see what he can come up with," Lucas added. "That Ms. Williams woke up in a hospital smacks of a cover-up. I have contacts in the local medical field. I'll sound those out…as well."

Patrick would wager Lucas Camp had contacts in most fields, most places.

Windy stood. "Thank you, sir, ma'am," she said to Lucas and Victoria.

Patrick assured Victoria that he and Windy would

check in periodically, before following his newly assigned partner from the office.

His first case.

He took a deep breath. He was ready to make this leap.

No more looking back.

*Downtown Women's Shelter*

PATRICK AND HIS PARTNER emerged from his sedan. He considered the neighborhood. Residential. Quiet. The trilevel house that served as a home for those who had no place to go looked like any other nearby. There were no posted signs or other indications that the address was any different from the rest that lined the immaculately maintained street.

But there was a major difference. This home protected the women who stayed there. A pass code was required for admittance. No official ID would serve the purpose. Your name was either on the entrance list and you possessed the necessary information or you didn't get in.

Period.

Abused and otherwise devastated women from all walks of life sought temporary refuge here. Their troubles would never find them here, nor would their abusers, whether friend or relative. This shelter was the most successful in all of Chicago at protecting its residents. Not one had been tracked down to this location.

Precisely why Lucas Camp had brought Sande Williams here.

Patrick stayed two steps behind Windy as they approached the house. The gate wasn't locked, but there would be an armed guard just inside the closed and secured door. There would be no getting past him without the proper authorization.

Windy knocked, then recited the necessary pass code. A couple of seconds later, no doubt after the guard had studied both Patrick and her through the cameras positioned on either end of the porch, the door opened for their admittance.

"Windy Millwood." The guard turned his attention to Patrick. "Patrick O'Brien."

Windy displayed her Colby Agency ID, as did Patrick.

"Welcome." The guard stepped back and allowed them to enter.

Inside, the long, narrow entrance hall was deserted. Before Patrick could assess the setting, a middle-aged woman stepped from the first door on the left.

"Your client is waiting in the conference room," she said before thrusting out her hand. "I'm Carlene Mitchell, the administrator."

"Windy Millwood." She shook the woman's hand. "And this is my colleague, Patrick O'Brien."

Patrick had from his first day at the Colby Agency insisted that the title of doctor be dropped. He offered his hand to their host. "We understand our presence here is an inconvenience. We appreciate your hospitality."

Carlene nodded, but her smile was noticeably restrained. "This way."

The administrator led the way to what had likely once been a grand dining room. Sande Williams waited there. She looked even younger than her photo and, quite frankly, scared to death. Her arms were crossed around her middle, and her shoulders shook, though she visibly struggled to control the outward display of weakness. Fear ultimately won the battle.

When the introductions had been made and Carlene had left them to their work, Windy began the interview. "Ms. Williams, why don't you start from the beginning and tell us what happened yesterday."

Seated across from her at the well-used dining table, Patrick analyzed the woman as she spoke. She repeated the story of waking outside the morgue and running for her life, for reasons she didn't understand. Sande Williams, although clearly nervous, stoically went over the details of her only memories. Anything beyond the past twenty-four hours was lost to her, a very rare phenomenon, but not completely unheard of. Patrick decided to reserve conclusions until after he'd spoken with her at length.

"Ms. Williams," he said when she'd finished her story, to the point where a kind man, Lucas Camp, had delivered her here, "putting the facts aside, how do you feel?"

She blinked, those wide blue eyes connecting fully with his for the first time. "What do you mean?"

He leaned back in his chair to further set a tone of relaxation. "You're nervous, I'm sure. That's to be expected. Any headaches? Dizziness? Anger or other feelings of emotion?"

Sande moved her head from side to side. "No. Well, I'm scared, but mostly I feel…disjointed. As if I've lost something that I don't know how to get back. Does that make sense?"

"Yes. It makes perfect sense." Classic disorientation response. "Do you feel apprehensive in our presence?" It was very important for her to trust those who were handling her case. They would get nowhere until she felt at ease in his and Windy's company.

"A little," she admitted. She moistened her lips and let go a big, shaky breath. "But I know I have to trust someone to help me. I can't do this alone."

That was a start. "Do you have any physical injuries?" Patrick saw no visible signs, but there could be bruises, lumps, bumps or scratches beneath her clothing.

She hesitated, as if pondering his question at length. "None that I've discovered."

"What about dreams?" He studied his client's face for those reactions she wouldn't put into words. "Did you have any dreams last night that you recall?"

Again, she shook her head. "None that I remember."

"You understand that Windy and I want to help you learn what happened to you prior to yesterday? We'll do everything we can to that end."

She gave a resolute nod. "Yes."

Now for the first big hurdle. "Then you won't mind accompanying us to the residence listed on your driver's license, in an attempt to prompt your memory."

Not a question.

She hesitated a beat, then two. "No…except I worry that *they'll* be watching."

"They?"

"Whoever…the people who did this to me." She wet her lips again. His gaze followed the movement despite his best intentions.

"That's an understandable fear," Windy assured her when he didn't immediately do so.

"It's our job to protect you from this moment forward. You understand that we'll do all within our power to that end?" Patrick watched for the slightest change in her expression, in her eyes.

"Yes." She drew in a deep, steadying breath. "Mr. Camp said that the people from the Colby Agency would do whatever necessary to ensure my safety while investigating my case."

"We will," Windy reiterated. "Whenever you're with Patrick or myself you'll have no reason to fear anyone. We're both highly trained and very good at what we do. You leave the worrying to us."

"What if I don't remember anything?" Sande looked from Patrick to Windy and back. "I mean, I don't know if Sande Williams is even my name." She shrugged. "The picture on the driver's license is definitely me. But it doesn't *feel* like me."

There was the possibility that this woman simply no longer wanted to be who she was. But that conclusion did not explain her waking up at a morgue with a sheet over her nude body and a toe tag attached to her foot. That part indicated foul play, without doubt.

"That's our job," Windy declared. "We'll find out who you are and why this has happened to you. We won't stop until we do."

Relief was evident in their new client's eyes, but

the worry remained. "I don't understand how this could have happened."

"There could," Patrick offered, "be psychological reasons for your amnesia." He turned his palms up. "There could be drugs involved. Many times when there is no physical trauma or psychological explanation, the cause of amnesia is drug related."

Her eyebrows knitted in confusion. "Drugs? You think I might have been involved with drugs?"

"Not the kind you think," he hastened to explain. "I'm referring to mind-altering drugs that might have been administered without your consent or your knowledge. Perhaps you agreed to partake in some sort of drug trial and are suffering a rare side effect. Our first stop today will be a private clinic. Our associate there will take the necessary samples and determine if you've recently been exposed to drugs."

Sande nodded. "And if we find something, what then?"

Windy picked up from there. "The hospital where you awoke insists you were never a patient in their facility. They have no record at all of you, they claim. But based on your story, you were a patient there, however briefly. Their denial gives us reason to suspect there's a cover-up of some sort going on."

"I don't remember how I got there or anything that happened before I woke up on that gurney." Sande closed her eyes for a long moment. "I don't understand how this could be happening." When her eyes opened, her gaze locked with Patrick's. "How could a person just lose all they were? It seems crazy."

He wouldn't say so just now, but there were a number of mental illnesses that presented with amnesia. Most often because the patient simply did not want to remember who she or he was. That diagnosis would take time, time spent with the patient.

"We'll operate under the assumption that you're a victim," Windy assured her. "Your safety will be our top priority during our investigation."

Sande Williams bit her bottom lip as the fingers of her right hand twisted and twirled a lock of her long blond hair. "But there is the possibility that I'm just plain crazy."

"Not crazy," Patrick corrected. "You may have suffered a psychotic break. Stress. Any number of triggers could have set off the episode. But that doesn't explain the hospital's denial of your presence in their facility. These are the questions we have to consider and find explanations for."

She contemplated his words before she spoke again. Looking directly at him, she asked, "But you'll fix whatever it is, right?"

Patrick infused all the reassurance he could into his gaze. "You have our word we will find the problem—" he leaned forward slightly for emphasis "—and will do whatever it takes to rectify that problem, or get you to the people who can."

Relief filled her eyes. "Thank you."

What he suddenly felt contradicted all that he had just stated to this woman. For the first time since he'd entered Victoria's office and learned of this assignment, Patrick had second thoughts.

Sande Williams was a complete mystery. A woman in serious trouble. Whatever demons, real or imagined, haunted her, he had promised that he would take care of her and the situation.

How the hell could he make that kind of assurance when he hadn't even really known his own wife? He had lived with her for years and hadn't experienced the slightest inkling that all was not as it should be. He'd failed her and he'd failed himself.

As if Windy sensed his mental retreat, she took the reins. "Ms. Williams, this is what we do at the Colby Agency, and we're very, very good at what we do. We will find the truth and take whatever steps are necessary to resolve your dilemma. You're in good hands."

On cue, Patrick felt a tremor.

Maybe he wasn't as ready for a field assignment as he'd thought.

This wasn't a mere compilation of facts and data to be passed along to an investigator for follow through. This involved dealing directly with the people of interest in the case.

*This* was the real thing.

# Chapter Three

2422 Johnson Lane
Chicago Suburb

"Here's how we're going to play this." The first part of the job would be no hardship for Patrick. He knew how to read people. "We approach—"

"Wait." Sande looked from him to the house across the street and back. "I'm not sure about this. What if I do or say the wrong thing?"

Fifteen minutes ago she had been fully prepared to participate in this phase of the investigation. No hesitation. The plan was simple. They would approach the residence listed on her driver's license and see if she recognized the place or anyone residing there. At the same time, he would be analyzing any occupants for recognition of his client. In and out in a matter of minutes. No big deal.

"Windy checked out the lady living here," he offered again, in hopes of calming Sande's fear. "She's a CPA. Single. And she has no criminal record, not even a parking ticket. She's lived here for three years. There's nothing to be worried about."

Sande cast another furtive glance at the house. "But what if she somehow knows the people who did this to me? What if she's involved?"

Her teeth tortured her bottom lip. He'd noticed she did that when she was nervous or uncertain. The need to protect stirred in him. Not unusual in this situation. She was vulnerable, he was not. Basic human compassion dictated that primal response. He'd tried to ignore going down that path for a few years now. But compassion was a necessary element of his interaction with the client. There was no discounting it now.

Patrick gazed at the ranch-style brick home across the street from where he'd parked along the curb. "Determining whether or not the lady of the house is involved is part of what we'll hopefully learn on this visit. Remember, we have the element of surprise on our side. She has no idea we're coming. She won't be prepared to cause trouble or set any sort of trap."

He wasn't sure he'd convinced Sande, but she hadn't flat out refused to go inside as of yet. He wondered if she would be more willing if a woman had been here. His associate was running Sande's fingerprints and doing additional research on the hospital where she had awakened on that gurney.

Patrick didn't need Windy for this step. He could handle an interview without his associate's guidance. *This* was his specialty. All he needed was the client's cooperation.

"Okay." Sande took a deep breath. "Let's do it."

He breathed a little easier with that decision out of the way.

They crossed the street side by side. His client's trepidation was palpable despite her determination to go through with this step. They had been watching the house for more than half an hour when the owner had come home. Since the woman had parked in the garage before emerging from her car, neither he nor Sande had been able to get a good look at her.

According to Windy's research, the owner was Nancy Childers. Other than her occupation, the fact that she had no criminal record and that she had moved to Chicago from Detroit, they knew nothing else. She appeared to be a loner and had no listed next of kin.

The instant Patrick and Sande reached the front door of the house, she turned to him, her eyes wide with worry again. "I don't say anything, right?"

"Exactly." They'd been over this already. "Study

the woman. The house. If you've been here before you may experience déjà vu or some emotional tug."

Sande took another of those deep, bolstering breaths as she nodded.

"Try to stay relaxed and just *feel*."

"I can do that."

Her voice sounded strong despite the uncertainty in her eyes. Patrick rapped on the door and waited. A second knock was required before it opened.

A female matching Nancy Childers's physical description looked expectantly from Patrick to Sande. "Can I help you?"

"Ms. Childers?"

The expected suspicion flashed in the woman's eyes. "Yes."

"My name is Patrick O'Brien, and this is my colleague, Sande Williams. We're canvassing the area regarding a problem with burglaries. Do you have five minutes to discuss the recent rash of incidents in your neighborhood?"

When looking for a cover story, he'd read about the outbreak of robberies in the area. Any criminal activity in the community was likely to prompt immediate cooperation from residents. And if Ms. Childers reacted as expected, she would automatically assume he represented the local authorities in one capacity or another.

Nancy Childers hesitated only half a second. "Sure." The suspicion vanished and she managed a polite smile. "Come in." The door opened wider in invitation as she stepped back, allowing them entrance.

"We can talk in the living room." She led the way.

When they were seated, Patrick explained briefly what he'd learned about the rash of robberies before asking, "Have you considered that someone in your neighborhood might be the perpetrator?"

Nancy frowned. "No." She shook her head. "I discussed the problem with one of my neighbors just yesterday and we're shocked. This isn't the norm for this area. I guess I'm lucky my home wasn't hit, since I'm rarely here."

"So you haven't noticed any suspicious activities? No strange automobiles or people loitering about?"

"No. Not at all."

"May I use your restroom?" Sande interjected.

No one was more surprised by the question than Patrick. He glanced from Sande, who'd asked, to their host.

Nancy's brow creased with another frown, this one laced with renewed suspicion. "Sure." She hesitated a second or two, then waved her hand in the direction of the hall. "Second door on the right."

When Sande had left the room, Patrick drew the woman's attention back to the conversation. "Are any of the residents in the neighborhood new arrivals? Or is there anyone who perhaps keeps a particularly low profile? You'd be surprised how important small, seemingly insignificant details like that can be to an investigation."

Nancy pondered his question. "It's difficult for me to say, since I travel so frequently. In fact, I only just returned from several weeks in Dallas."

"Your work keeps you away for extended periods?" She'd mentioned that, but he wanted details.

"Most of the time." She shifted to a more relaxed position, but the tightening of her jaw gave away her continued uneasiness. "I help analyze and organize accounting departments for major corporations."

So far he'd learned nothing he didn't already know. Once he and Sande were gone, the woman's actions would tell the rest of the story—if there was anything else to tell.

Noting Sande's approach from the hall, Patrick stood. "We certainly appreciate your cooperation, Ms. Childers. If you think of anything at all out of the ordinary that you might have forgotten to mention, please give me a call." He provided her with a card that included his name and cell-phone number. "One of us will be in touch if we think of any additional questions."

Sande resumed her position at his side, her expression as neutral as it had been when they first entered the house. She shook Nancy's hand and thanked her for her cooperation. Patrick studied the interaction between the two women. Nothing. Not a flicker of recognition.

Nancy Childers was either an accomplished actress or a dead end.

Patrick didn't question his client until the door was closed behind them and they were nearing the street. "Nothing, huh?"

Sande shook her head. "Nothing."

"Sande!"

Patrick's attention jerked left, toward the source of the greeting. An older woman, seventy or seventy-five, waved from the yard next door to Nancy Childers's home. As he watched, she leaned her rake against the fence, tugged off her gloves and started in their direction.

"I thought that was you!" The spry woman hurried to the sidewalk to meet them. "I've missed our garden chats. Where in the world have you been?" She scrutinized Sande for longer than was comfortable. "You don't look well. Have you been ill?"

Sande's expression left no question as to her utter surprise as well as total confusion. "I…uh, yes. I've been in the hospital."

The older lady shook her head. "I wish you'd

called me. I didn't know what in the world happened. Then those men came around this morning looking for you, and I didn't know what to say. They wouldn't tell me a thing, just kept asking questions." She wrung her hands. "Frankly, I was worried you'd…" She looked left then right, as if expecting trouble from somewhere on the street. "There are so many murders these days." She heaved out a big breath. "You never know when someone just disappears like that. I sure wish you'd called."

"I'm sorry." Patrick offered his hand, diverting her attention to him. "I don't think we've met. I'm Patrick O'Brien."

"Alma Spears." She grasped his hand with surprising strength. "I keep a watch on Nancy's house when she's away. Usually." Her gaze shifted back to Sande. "But this time she hired herself a house sitter while she was away. I was going to ask her about that, but every time I drop by she's on her way out or tied up on the phone." Alma glanced back at the house. "Maybe she thinks I'm getting too old for the job." Alma smiled. "In the end I made myself a new friend in Sande here." Her smile dimmed. "I'm so glad to see you're all right."

Sande stared at the woman who called herself Alma Spears. She'd said one thing that had settled like a massive stone in her stomach. "Men came looking for me?" The idea that it may have been those men from the hospital who'd come here terrified her.

"Yes. Two of 'em." Alma dabbed at her forehead with the back of her hand. "If you're not in a hurry, why don't you come on in and we'll visit over some tea?" She made eye contact with Mr. O'Brien. "Or coffee."

Two men. More of that paralyzing fear prickled Sande's skin. *Wait. Focus.* The woman had asked her a question. Tea. She wanted to visit. Maybe that was a good idea. How was it that this Alma Spears could know Sande? And she felt no sense of recognition? No connection whatsoever?

"Coffee would be great," O'Brien agreed cordially.

Sande had to pay attention. She'd completely ignored the invitation. *Pull it together, girl.* O'Brien had told her to pay attention. To relax and just feel.

Alma Spears led the way through her backyard, past a lush garden. Lots of pansies and deep-green ferns set against the darkening red of dwarf nandinas.

Once inside, she said, "You two make yourselves at home and I'll get the refreshments."

As soon as Alma was out of earshot, O'Brien turned to Sande. "You're certain nothing in the house next door stirred even the slightest reaction?"

She shook her head. "I explored a bit when I asked to use the restroom. Nothing felt familiar." That was the absolute worst feeling. To know you had a history, maybe family, and not be able to access those memories. It was like some part of her—the part that mattered the most—was missing.

"What about this lady?" he prodded. "Anything?"

Sande turned her palms up. "Nothing yet."

His next question was preempted by Alma's return. The tray she carried was laden with a floral porcelain coffeepot and three dainty cups and saucers. "I was hoping we'd get to say a proper goodbye before you left for your next assignment." She passed Sande a cup prepared with tea, then filled the remaining two with coffee before passing one to O'Brien. "After four days I was certain you weren't coming back." She cradled her own cup and sighed. "Like I said before, I feared the worst."

"Did the men who came looking for Ms. Williams identify themselves?" O'Brien sipped his coffee as nonchalantly as if he'd just asked if there might be rain in the forecast.

Alma gestured to a small plate of cookies on the tray, but both Sande and O'Brien declined. "I guess I should've asked for ID," the woman admitted, "but they seemed so official. I was worried that something had happened and they just weren't telling me one way or the other. I got a little snippy toward the end of their visit."

Sande stared at her, stunned. Four days? She had been missing for four days? This was unbelievable.

"Did either one of the men who visited you mention the recent rash of burglaries in your neighborhood?" O'Brien asked, keeping up the pretense, or just making conversation so as not to arouse suspicion, Sande supposed.

The exchange continued on benignly about what a great neighborhood Alma lived in, how she had known everyone on the street for ages. Sande sat stone still, utterly dumbfounded, while she then chatted on and on about her garden, and the relationship the two of them had seemingly developed.

"You're sure it was only two months ago that Sande moved in next door?" O'Brien looked to Sande. "I was thinking three?"

Before Sande could decide what he wanted her to say, Alma shook her head with complete confidence. "Absolutely not. It was Labor Day weekend. You said you didn't know a soul in the neighborhood and that Nancy wouldn't be back for several more weeks."

"Wait. Yes," O'Brien allowed, "I think you're right. Nancy had to go to Dallas."

Alma's forehead furrowed. "Dallas? I thought she was in San Diego?" She turned to Sande then, a mix of confusion and suspicion in her eyes. "You took her place at the firm here while she did your work out in

San Diego. I'm sure that's what you told me." Her head wagged again. "I'll never understand this whole life-swap thing. People don't like to take risks anymore. They want to try everything out before they make a commitment."

Total numbness had overtaken Sande. Life swapping? What was she talking about?

Alma studied her for a long moment. "You act like you don't even recall staying here. Are you sure you're all right?"

Sande froze. How did she respond to that?

"Sande was quite ill," O'Brien interjected quickly. "The medication has made the past few days a little hazy."

The older woman nodded in understanding, but her expression indicated she was less than convinced of their story.

Fear snaked its way up Sande's spine. What if the woman called those men back and told them she had been here? Had they given Alma Spears a card? She hadn't mentioned that, but maybe she'd been asked not to say anything. Confusion and fear had wrapped around Sande in so many layers she couldn't draw a breath. Her heart thumped hard against her sternum.

After a few minutes more casual back and forth, they had obviously extracted all they were going to get from Alma Spears. They had learned that Sande supposedly filled in for Nancy at Peyton and Wyatt, an accounting firm in Chicago where Nancy was employed. Maybe someone at the firm would recognize Sande. Would know where she'd lived before coming to Chicago. Would remember if she had any family or friends.

"Thank you, Alma." Sande produced a shaky smile as she used the woman's first name in hopes of not rousing more suspicion. She suddenly couldn't wait to get out of the woman's house. Being there felt strange…disconcerting. The more the woman said the less real any of it felt to her. She needed air.

Once back on the sidewalk, she drew in a deep, ragged breath. She felt dazed and even more confused than when they had arrived. "This is impossible. Her story can't be true."

O'Brien escorted her to his car. "First thing we do is find out where Nancy Childers has really been the past two months. And if you actually filled in for her at Peyton and Wyatt."

"We're going to talk to her again?" Sande wished she felt something, even the slightest flicker of recognition, where Nancy Childers was concerned. But there was nothing. Not a single thing about Alma Spears felt familiar, either. If Sande had ever met one or the other, she had absolutely no recall.

"Not yet." O'Brien opened the front passenger

door of his sedan. "But we will talk to both those ladies again, count on it."

One thing kept Sande hanging on at this point. Lucas Camp had said the Colby Agency was the very best in the business.

She had to believe that.

She had to believe in something.

## Chapter Four

Patrick braked for a stop sign at the end of the street. Sande's anxiety radiated off her in waves. There wasn't much he could say to console her that he hadn't already. Only time and the slowly unraveling mystery of her identity would give her the peace she needed.

Though he had worked with only one patient with this level of amnesia, he sympathized with the fears and insecurities she no doubt experienced. He'd suffered a few of those himself when he'd first come on board at the Colby Agency.

He pulled his phone from his jacket pocket and put in a call to Windy, getting directly to the point. "We need a more in-depth background search on Nancy Childers."

In answer to his partner's prompt regarding Sande's reaction to the woman and the residence, he kept his answer concise so as not to unnerve their client any more than she already was. "None."

When his passenger turned to stare out the car window, he understood that she hadn't been fooled.

As he drove through the intersection, he brought Windy up to speed about the neighbor, Alma Spears. "Let's get some background information on her, as well."

After hearing her promise that she would get moving on the two women, as well as the Peyton and Wyatt firm, he ended the call and put his phone away. Sande continued staring out at the passing landscape. There were few reassurances he could give her, but he could fill her in on his plan. That would at least give her hope.

"We should have something preliminary on the background searches in a few hours." When she didn't respond, he added, "Until then, if you'd like to stop for an early lunch, we can do that."

She turned toward him. He glanced from the street to her and back, but even in that brief moment he recognized the anger that had replaced the fear.

"No. I want to go to the firm, Peyton and Wyatt. I need to know if they can confirm Alma Spears's story."

He couldn't blame her for not wanting to wait for Windy's report. Still, the company was an unknown element. Patrick drove another block or so as he weighed the possible ramifications to his client, and the trouble they could run into. Both were irrelevant to some degree. If he were in Sande's shoes he would do the same thing. The waiting was the worst part.

"Let me make a couple of calls first."

He would get the street address from Windy and then do a little recon before taking Sande there. No matter how frustrated she was waiting, her safety had to be paramount.

For the second time today his confidence took a tumble.

Profiling suspects and persons of interest was one thing, field investigation and personal security quite another. The crime scene photos from his wife's murder flashed before his eyes. He hadn't been able to protect the woman he married. How could he possibly trust himself to protect anyone else?

SANDE STARED at the towering skyscraper. Peyton and Wyatt was housed on an upper floor of a prestigious building right on the Magnificent Mile. Wouldn't she remember if she'd been here before?

Wouldn't she feel something?

How was it possible that absolutely nothing looked or felt familiar to her?

She closed her eyes and summoned the reflection of herself she'd studied in the mirror of the ladies' room at the shelter.

Kind of short, small frame. Blond hair, blue eyes.

Where had she been born? Where had she attended school? College? First job? First boyfriend? Did she have a best friend? Any siblings?

Nothing came to mind. Not a face or name or place. Nothing.

Sande opened her eyes and stared at the unfamiliar building once more. Had she worked here for two months? Were there people in the building who knew her?

"Are you ready?"

Patrick O'Brien's voice tugged her attention in his direction. The concern on his face was genuine. But there was more. Uncertainty? Maybe. He was very difficult to read. There was something about him that made her feel safe. Or maybe it was just the idea that he worked at the Colby Agency, and her only friend, the homeless box lady named Madge, had seemed so certain the agency could help her.

Intelligence emanated from his brown eyes. He was tall, broad shouldered, and looked quite strong and capable. Even his name sounded dependable.

Patrick O'Brien.

He had promised to keep her safe. To find her lost past. She had to count on that. No second-guessing, no hesitation.

"Yes," she said finally. "I'm ready."

He indicated that she should precede him. He was a gentleman, too. Always opened the car door for her and insisted she go first. His wife was a lucky woman. Instinctively, Sande glanced at his left hand. No ring. Maybe he didn't have a wife.

Where in the world had that thought come from?

Did *she* have a husband?

She was allowing her thoughts to wander off in foolish territory. If she had a husband, she would be wearing a ring. Unless it had been removed along with her clothes at the hospital.

What did it matter, anyway? How would she know what kind of husband she had or would prefer, when she didn't even know who she was? Enough stalling. Drawing a calming breath, she headed for the main entrance of the building where she had supposedly worked the past couple of months. O'Brien stayed close behind her, as if he sensed her trepidation without her having to say a word. She liked that he seemed to understand how she felt and what she needed.

Then again, maybe she was developing that strange syndrome people got when they became attached to their abductors. She felt exactly like a lost puppy following around the only human who had bothered to feed her.

The marble-floored lobby soared two stories high and encompassed the entire first floor. Windows rose to meet that grand height, filling the space with light. Trees and lush potted plants lent a welcoming atmosphere to the elaborate decorating. Inviting upholstered chairs held court near the reception desk.

And yet not one thing about the place looked or felt familiar to Sande. Three strikes. Did that mean she was out?

O'Brien approached the desk and spoke to the security guard on duty. Sande surveyed the extensive atrium a second, then a third time, hoping to spot anything that might stimulate her memory.

Since she possessed no identification other than the printout from the DMV, O'Brien had to do some fancy talking to get her on the visitors log. When badges were finally issued, they boarded the elevator for the top floor.

Sande started to speak, but O'Brien leaned close and whispered in her ear. "Not now."

At first she didn't understand what he meant, then realized that there was every likelihood the elevator as well as the entire building was monitored for security purposes. Anything she might say could be overheard. A new blast of fear sent goose bumps rushing over her skin. Could those men who had chased her from the hospital, who had asked Alma Spears about her, work here?

O'Brien knew what he was doing. *Relax,* she

ordered herself. All she had to do was follow his lead. He would take care of her.

Thank God, because she was flying blind.

The elevator glided to a stop and the doors opened silently.

*Big breath.* Sande stepped off the elevator, O'Brien close behind her. At the receptionist's desk, he moved up beside her.

"Good morning. I'm Patrick O'Brien and this is Sande Williams."

The receptionist looked at both of them. For a split second Sande was certain the woman recognized her. It was nothing more than the slightest hesitation in returning her gaze to O'Brien, but there was definitely a hesitation. Hope bloomed in Sande's chest. This could be it.

"Do you have an appointment, Mr. O'Brien?"

"We're here to see…" O'Brien pulled his cell phone from his pocket and checked the screen "…Marsha Patton."

Evidently Windy had sent the name to him via a text message, because he hadn't received a call since asking her to check out Peyton and Wyatt.

The receptionist glanced at her computer, then settled her attention back on O'Brien. "I'm sorry, sir, but Mrs. Patton has a full schedule today. I can take your card and have her get back to you."

Sande's heart rate sped up. She couldn't wait until tomorrow or the day after that. How the heck was she supposed to figure out who she really was and where she'd come from if anyone who knew anything useful didn't cooperate?

Frustration chased away the last of the fear. Damn it. She needed help! Didn't anyone understand?

"Excuse me," she said firmly. The receptionist stared up at her, seemingly a little startled herself. "This won't wait. I need to see Marsha today. Now. Tell her Sande Williams will be waiting right over there." She pointed to the small seating area.

With that announcement she walked over to one of the chairs and sat down.

O'Brien said something to the receptionist, who looked flustered or worried or both. Then he joined Sande. "Good job," he murmured, leaning his head toward hers.

A tiny smile tugged at her lips. She might not have a clue who the heck she was, but she was finished with wallowing in that overwhelming feeling of helplessness. "Thanks."

He turned to look directly at her. "Any flickers of recognition?"

She shook her head. "I did get the impression the receptionist recognized me, though."

He nodded. "I picked up on that, too."

Before Sande's breathing had returned to some semblance of normal, a woman entered the reception area from the long corridor of offices beyond.

"Ms. Williams?"

Sande stared at her for a long moment. Dark hair, green eyes. Tall, thin. Seriously uptight-looking. She wore her hair pinned up in a no-fuss manner and her eyeglasses were practical wire frames.

Sande felt not a single flicker of recognition.

O'Brien stood. "Ms. Patton, I'm Patrick O'Brien."

Belatedly, Sande pushed herself to her feet. She blinked, tried not to continue staring at the woman who acted as if she did not know her. And whom Sande had no substantiated reason to believe she had ever seen before.

"I'm Marsha Patton, operations chief of Peyton and Wyatt." A professional smile slid into place. "Why don't we talk in my office?" She looked from Patrick to Sande, lingered only a moment or two before refocusing her attention on him.

When she turned to head back down the corridor, Patrick touched Sande's elbow and ushered her along in her wake. He had watched Marsha Patton's reaction closely as she'd scrutinized both of them. Unfortunately, he had noted little that indicated she had ever met Sande before, other than an almost imperceptible hesitation. But the receptionist, that was a different story. She had definitely recognized her.

Ms. Patton led the way to her spacious corner office. She indicated the two upholstered chairs in front of her gleaming desk and then settled into the tufted leather one on the other side.

"Your request seemed rather urgent. So…" she clasped her hands in front of her and relaxed into her chair "…how can I help you this morning?" She peered first at Sande, then at Patrick.

"Ms. Williams," he began, taking a shot in the dark, "is looking into her legal recourses related to her employment at your firm these past couple of months." Beside him Sande shifted uncomfortably. He hoped she would keep her cool and go along with him on this.

A frown furrowed Ms. Patton's brow. "I'm not sure I understand." She glanced at Sande again. "I've worked at this firm for five years, and until the two of you arrived a few moments ago, I've never heard the name Sande Williams before."

If the woman was lying she was quite good at the game of deceit. *Like his wife.*

Patrick banished the thought and focused his full attention on the woman behind the desk. "Let's not go the denial route, Mrs. Patton. Ms. Williams has a legitimate grievance and it would be easier for all concerned if this matter were settled quietly."

The slightest hint of apprehension appeared in Patton's firm expression, but she quickly schooled the reaction. "Perhaps I've not made myself clear," she suggested. "Ms. Williams is not, nor has she been, an employee of this firm. I cannot imagine what either of you hope to gain by this preposterous assertion."

"Well." Patrick rose to his full height. "In that case, perhaps we'll take our evidence to a criminal attorney and start from there."

No visible reaction this time. Marsha Patton picked up a business card from the display tray on her desk and handed it to him. "If your attorney has any questions, he or she may feel free to call me directly."

Patrick accepted the card, then escorted Sande from the office. He kept a loose grasp on her elbow until they were aboard the elevator and moving downward. When she looked at him, frustration written all over her face, he shook his head in a silent warning. They couldn't talk until they were out of the building.

Two minutes later they were on the sidewalk and headed for the car. "I know that receptionist recognized me," she insisted. "And I think that Patton woman did, too." She had to be lying.

Patrick opened the passenger door for her. "I got the same impression but that doesn't mean she *knows* you. As for Patton, my gut says she lied, but, if she did, she was damned good at it."

"She knows me," Sande argued as she dropped into the seat. "They both do."

He closed the door and rounded the hood. When he'd settled behind the steering wheel, he met her frustrated gaze. "You could have belonged to the same yoga class as the receptionist."

"I don't do yoga."

He started the car. "Are you sure about that?"

Staring straight ahead, arms crossed over her chest, she kept her lips pressed tightly together. Of course she couldn't remember, but she was too furious to admit it right now.

"Maybe you shared the same hairstylist," he offered, despite her silence.

She opened her mouth to deny that suggestion as well, but just as quickly closed it.

"There are hundreds of possibilities, none of which you would remember," he reminded her gently, knowing it was not what she wanted to hear. "However, if Patton is hiding something as I suspect, our visit will have done its job."

Sande waited until he'd eased into the flow of traffic and glanced back at her before asking, "How?"

"She or someone in the firm will react, attempt to figure out what we're up to, or how to stop us."

"Oh."

Judging by the uncertainty crammed into that one

word, Sande Williams hadn't considered the latter. "That's what we want them to do," he explained. "Without some sort of reaction from someone, we'll keep spinning our wheels and getting nowhere."

"What do we do now? Just wait?"

He started to clarify that yes, they would be waiting, though that wouldn't stop their investigation into other avenues. But the dark sedan in his rearview mirror suddenly gave him pause. That same vehicle had matched their last three turns.

Patrick took an abrupt left.

The black or navy sedan did the same.

He sped up.

So did the car behind him.

Driver and one passenger, both male, he noted as the car moved in closer and closer to his rear bumper.

Patrick pressed the accelerator more firmly. "Maybe we won't have to wait."

## Chapter Five

Sande gripped the armrest as the car charged forward.

She held her breath.

O'Brien swerved left to avoid a too-close encounter with the vehicle directly in front of them. He cut in front of the car he'd passed and rushed forward.

If one of the pedestrians on the sidewalk stepped off the curb…

No sooner had the thought formed than a woman moved toward the crosswalk.

Sande gasped.

O'Brien hit the brakes.

The car skidded to a hard, jarring stop mere inches from the pedestrian, who had frozen in her tracks.

Silence vibrated inside the vehicle, and Sande's heart bumped back into a frantic rhythm.

"You okay?"

She managed a jerky nod.

Then O'Brien did the last thing she expected; he put the car in Park, opened his door and climbed out. Before she could say a word, he'd stormed up to the vehicle idling behind them. The very same car that had been chasing them.

What the heck was he doing?

Twisting around in the seat, Sande watched as O'Brien waltzed right up to the driver's door and said something through the window. Abruptly, the car backed up, cut around him and roared away.

Horns blasted at both the car speeding off and the one in which Sande sat, parked at the crosswalk and blocking an entire lane of traffic. O'Brien slid back behind the wheel.

"What did you do?" Sande glared at him. "That was…" She struggled to find the right word. "That was dangerous!"

He put the car in Drive and rolled forward. "Not really. I asked him a simple question."

Was he trying to get himself run over or killed?

O'Brien glanced at her. "I asked him if I could help him."

"You're kidding, right?" Sande checked all directions to make sure the car wasn't coming back.

"Nope."

Her gaze settled on O'Brien once more. "What did he say?"

"That's when he drove away."

She shook her head. "You could've been shot or run over or something!" Did all Colby investigators take those kinds of risks? He could have been killed! He wouldn't be able to help her if he was dead. Good grief!

He lifted one shoulder in a shrug. "It's daylight. The street was crowded, so there were lots of witnesses." He checked the left lane before easing into it. "And there was a police cruiser half a dozen cars behind us."

The words were scarcely out of his mouth before she turned around to check. Sure enough, the cop car was still there, three or four cars behind.

She relaxed. Okay, so maybe he had known what he was doing. Sande closed her eyes and released a heavy breath. She had to trust someone. It might as well be him. Hadn't she already decided that? *Stay on track, girl. This is too important to be wishy-washy.*

The buzz of a cell phone interrupted her thoughts. He reached into the pocket of his jacket and withdrew his phone.

"O'Brien."

Sande considered his profile as he listened to the caller. Strong jaw. Firm mouth. Good hands, too, she noted as she studied the one holding the phone. He looked…reliable.

She shook her head. Hadn't she already had this conversation with herself?

He closed the phone and tucked it back into his pocket. "That was Windy."

Anticipation zinged along Sande's nerve endings. "Has she found something?" That would be a step in the right direction. At this point Sande would be thrilled to hear any news about her past or the results of the drug test, good, bad or indifferent.

"We have to return to Nancy Childers's home."

"Has she changed her mind about knowing me?" That would be an about-face. Or maybe Alma had called with additional information.

"Not exactly."

There was something different in O'Brien's tone this time. Sande couldn't quite label the inflection, but whatever it was made her uneasy. "What do you mean? If she doesn't want to talk, why are we going back?"

He braked for a traffic light, then his gaze settled on hers. "Nancy Childers is dead, Sande."

"Dead?" But they'd spoken with her just a few hours ago. Two, maybe three. How could she be dead? "What happened?"

"I don't have details. All I know is that Alma Spears decided to pay her a visit. She found the front door ajar."

Dread coiled in Sande's stomach. "Nancy Childers

was murdered." Not a question. She knew deep in her gut that the woman had been *murdered*. The word tasted bitter on her tongue.

"Yes."

Had Nancy Childers been murdered because they'd visited her? Was her killer someone trying to track down Sande? What a foolish question. Of course that was the reason the woman was dead.

Sande leaned back in her seat and fought the overwhelming emotions.

Not only was someone after her, they obviously wanted her dead.

How was she supposed to fight an enemy she couldn't identify? Couldn't hope to recognize? With a past she couldn't remember?

If the bad guys were that close on her tail, how long would it be before they caught her in just the right situation?

Not long.

She twisted around and stared through the rear windshield. Prayed none of the cars on the street were following them like before. That chase had been just the beginning. The realization shuddered through her.

O'Brien had wanted a reaction. Sande was reasonably sure murder wasn't the one he had been hoping for. It certainly wasn't the one she'd wanted.

*2422 Johnson Lane*

DEFINITELY NOT the reaction Patrick had hoped for.

The brief car chase had been more than enough excitement for one day. A murder was way over the top. Particularly this early in the investigation.

If Sande Williams had been involved with people who thought nothing of killing a woman for simply talking to her, they were in for a hell of a bumpy ride.

Again he asked himself if he was up to this challenge. Might as well be. He was here. The client was here. He parked the car and got out. Giving up too early was not in his nature.

The last thing he wanted to do, however, was endanger Sande Williams. He glanced at her as she joined him at the front of the car. She was counting on him. Windy was counting on him.

Patrick surveyed the scene, silently steeled himself and pushed the uncertainty away. He could handle this.

Blue lights throbbed around the house where Nancy Childers had lived until a few hours ago. The array of official vehicles ranged from police to rescue squad and finally the coroner. The last stirred memories he'd prefer stay buried.

Windy waited at her car, well beyond the yellow tape that had been draped around the perimeter of the property. Alma Spears peered out a side window.

Patrick's gaze collided with hers just before she allowed the blind to snap back into place.

He had a feeling that lady knew far more than she was telling. Or maybe she was just afraid.

"My contact in homicide," Windy said as she approached them, "said the victim had one shot to the back of the head. Ballistics will take awhile, but he's guessing a silencer was used, since none of the neighbors appeared to have heard anything."

"No sign of forced entry?" Patrick studied the proximity of the houses in the neighborhood. That someone had driven up to the home and walked in without drawing attention indicated the deceased hadn't put up a fuss. Had Nancy Childers recognized her killer?

"No forced entry. Techs are lifting prints and trace evidence now, but it's doubtful they'll find anything connected to the killer."

One shot to the back of the head. Most likely a professional hit. The killer would have used gloves and would have been in and out in a matter of minutes, if not seconds. Windy was right; there would be no evidence. Ballistics probably wouldn't give them anything, either, with the exception of whether or not a silencer was used.

Patrick considered the client waiting next to him. Odds were that this murder was about her. Bringing her to the scene was a risk. If the killer or killers were still hanging around the neighborhood, she would be spotted. The sheer trauma could create additional psychological problems for her.

And yet exposure was the only way to trigger repressed memories.

Unless they went the hypnosis route, and that was another risky method.

He would need to discuss it with Sande. The stakes had been seriously raised with this murder, not to mention the car chase, however short-lived.

He glanced at the window where he'd noticed Alma Spears peering out. "I think we'll pay the neighbor another visit." He looked back at Windy. "Let me know if you learn anything else from your contact."

She withdrew her cell phone and checked the screen. "Will do."

As Patrick and Sande headed for the house next door he heard Windy answer her cell. They were expecting results from the lab, but it was too early for that. Maybe tomorrow.

"Excuse me! Hold up one moment, sir!"

Patrick stopped and turned to face the man who had called out to him. Not a uniform, but definitely a cop. The trench coat if not the cigarette dangling from the corner of his mouth gave him away.

Patrick prepared for the usual territory battle.

"Patrick O'Brien." He extended his hand. "How can I help you?"

The cop shot a quick look at Sande, then met Patrick's gaze as he reached to shake his hand. "Detective Carl Lyons. You're with the Colby Agency?"

Patrick nodded. "That's right."

Lyons jerked his head in Windy's direction. "You're with her?"

"Right again." Patrick braced for the next question.

"And this is…" Lyons gestured toward Sande.

"Sande Williams." She didn't offer her hand. Her expression announced just exactly how terrified she was at the moment.

Lyons nodded as he considered the name. "Did you know the victim?"

Sande glanced at Patrick before answering. "No."

The cop bobbed his head again. "Really?"

Patrick's instincts went on alert. "We have an interview to conduct, Detective Lyons. Do you have specific questions?"

Lyons studied him for several seconds before responding. "We'd like to talk to Ms. Williams downtown. Will that be a problem?"

"Not a problem at all." Patrick gently grasped Sande's elbow, primarily because she looked ready to bolt. "We can go now or later. Whatever's convenient for you, Detective."

That probing gaze searched Patrick's again. "Don't you want to know why we'd like to speak with her?"

Another warning fired in Patrick's veins. "If you're prepared to discuss the matter now, sure. We can do it here."

Lyons took a final drag from his cigarette, then tossed it to the street and smashed it with the toe of his shoe. "Why not?" He looked from Patrick to Sande and back. "Ms. Williams is wanted in D.C. for identity theft." His attention settled on her once more. "We're going to need to straighten out this matter and any possible connection to the victim." He hitched a thumb toward the Childers's home. "The neighbor, a Ms. Alma Spears, told us the two of you had visited the victim today."

"That's correct. However, Ms. Williams was not acquainted with the victim," Patrick countered. "Ms. Childers said as much during our visit."

Lyons retrieved a pack of cigarettes from his coat pocket and tapped one out. "I find that very strange, since Nancy Childers was also using a stolen identity, and charges are pending against her in D.C. as well." He shrugged. "Maybe it's just one big coincidence."

Patrick started to argue, since a background check had been run on Sande Williams as well as Nancy Childers that very morning, and nothing had been found. No pending charges, nothing. But protesting at this point without evidence would be pointless. He would need the printout Windy had pulled that morning.

"I've never been to D.C.," Sande interjected, her voice small and uncertain.

Lyons shrugged, then lit his cigarette. "Maybe not. We can clear that up easily enough. Why don't I meet you at the precinct and get this settled so there's no more confusion?"

"I'll check in with my associate," Patrick offered, "and then we'll come straight to you."

The cop's gaze narrowed. "What about your interview?"

"My associate can handle that."

Another one of those careless shrugs lifted the detective's shoulders. "Half hour. I'll be looking for you." Detective Lyons did an about-face and headed back to his crime scene.

"I thought the Colby Agency did a background search on me."

Patrick kept an eye on Lyons until he'd disappeared into the victim's home. "We did. There was nothing there."

Sande considered the doorway that Lyons had entered, then met Patrick's eyes again. "How is that possible?"

"I don't know." He surveyed the street and the

signs screaming that a crime had been committed in the vicinity. "But I will find out." He met his client's eyes. "You have my word on that."

The priority of the moment was keeping Sande Williams a free woman. If Lyons attempted to detain her, and succeeded, that would make this investigation exponentially more complicated.

# Chapter Six

If Sande had had any questions about the Colby Agency's influence, she had none now.

Detective Carl Lyons had wanted to detain her as a person of interest in his case as soon as she arrived at the precinct. Victoria Colby-Camp had made a single phone call and that idea had been nixed in a heartbeat.

No matter; Lyons had insisted on a thorough interview.

"Just stay calm and answer the questions to the best of your ability," O'Brien assured her again.

But that was the thing. She couldn't answer any questions because she had no idea what had happened in her life prior to about thirty-six hours ago.

Before she could say as much to O'Brien, Lyons entered the room with three cups of coffee. The detective settled a cup on the table in front of him, then offered the one in his right hand to Sande.

She shook her head. "I don't like coffee."

O'Brien held up a palm. "None for me, thanks."

Sande watched Lyon's response, but her mind was stalled on the one she'd made. The reaction had been instinctive. Alma Spears had served her tea, but Sande hadn't thought anything of it. She'd been too caught up in the idea that she had been missing, according to Alma, for four days. And that two men had come looking for her.

But now, with the detective's offer, the one thing Sande knew with absolute certainty was that she did not like coffee. Alma had known that.

Did that mean her memory was coming back? Would she recall some trivial something whenever her mind opted to allow a tiny fragment of the past to surface? Could it be that simple?

She prayed to God it would be.

When she snapped back to the present, Detective Lyons had already taken a seat and was analyzing her far too closely for comfort.

He set his coffee aside and leaned back in his chair, not allowing that probing gaze to waver an iota. "When did you move from D.C.?"

Sande glanced at O'Brien. He nodded. She was to answer to the best of her ability. Okay. That was easy enough. There was nothing to tell. "I have no recall of ever having lived in D.C."

The detective's eyebrows winged upward. "Is that so?"

"Yes."

"When did you move to Chicago?"

Sande moistened her lips and did what she had no choice but to do. She told the truth. "I have no idea, Detective Lyons. Who I was or what I did prior to yesterday morning is gone. I don't remember anything at all."

Eyes tapered with mounting doubt, Lyons took another long sip of his coffee. "You don't remember a thing, you say?"

Sande shook her head. "Nothing."

He turned his attention to O'Brien. "You believe her story?"

"I do." He stared the detective directly in the eyes. "Ms. Williams came to the Colby Agency requesting help in determining her identity. We're attempting to piece together her past. The driver's license and social security number are the extent of what we've been able to find so far. We visited Childers's residence only because that was the address listed on the driver's license issued to my client."

Lyons spread his arms wide. "I'm gonna be right up front with you, O'Brien. In all my years on the force, I've never encountered a real amnesia case. It's usually fake. Do you really expect me to believe that your client has no idea who she is or where she comes from?" He snorted. "Gimme a break."

Patrick chose his words carefully. "I expect you to understand that what my client is telling you is the truth to the best of her knowledge."

His fatigue showing for the first time, Lyons rubbed at his eyes with his thumb and forefinger, then leveled his gaze on Sande once more. "Then it's safe to assume you don't know if you stole someone else's identity back in D.C.? Or if you murdered the vic Nancy Childers, for that matter?"

Before Sande could protest, O'Brien spoke up. "Ms. Williams has been in my presence without exception since early this morning. Ms. Childers was very much alive when we left her today."

"Detective Lyons," Sande interjected. She needed more details. O'Brien had tiptoed around the issue when discussing it with the detective, probably to avoid the possibility of self-incrimination on her part. But Sande wanted all the details. She needed to know. "Can you be a little clearer about what happened in D.C.? I'm not sure I understand exactly what went on there. What is it you are accusing me of?"

Again Lyons scrutinized her at length, then said, "I'm not at liberty to disclose those details at this time."

"Wait!" That wasn't fair. Sande wanted to scream! "You can't do that."

A rap on the door drew the detective's attention and prevented his having to respond to Sande. Another detective, one she had been introduced to, but whose name she couldn't recall just now, stepped into the room. He passed Lyons a single sheet of paper and then slipped out again.

Lyons reviewed what appeared to be a report or lengthy note. When he lifted his attention to Sande once more he offered another of those careless shrugs. "I guess we can talk about those details, after all."

"Is there a reason you can talk about the case now when you couldn't two minutes ago?" O'Brien asked, his tone openly impatient.

Reaching across the table, Lyons passed the report to O'Brien. "Sure. Your client is not the woman we're looking for. The prints don't match."

Patrick scanned the report. Detective Lyons was correct. The Sande Williams accused of identity theft in D.C. was not the woman sitting next to Patrick. He met the detective's gaze. "Do you have a description of the Sande Williams suspected of committing this crime?"

"Absolutely." Lyons stood. "Give me a minute."

When the detective had left the interview room, Sande evidently couldn't hold back her frustration any longer. "What's going on?" Her blue eyes searched Patrick's, her worry and uncertainty crystal clear.

That was a question he couldn't answer. "I'm not sure. But I'm guessing the suspect's description is quite similar to yours, otherwise we wouldn't be here right now." He stared at the report, which basically told him nothing at all. "I've got a feeling the detective is as much in the dark as we are."

The door opened and Detective Lyons returned with a brown case file in hand. He settled into his chair and took his time going through the papers in the folder. When he no doubt felt confident the tension had mounted sufficiently, he pulled a photograph from among the pages and passed it to Patrick.

"This *was* Sande Williams."

Patrick accepted the photograph, held it loosely between his fingers as he stared, unblinking. At first, the image of his murdered wife transposed itself over the victim lying on the cold, stainless steel table with nothing more than a plain white sheet draping her nude body. Sweat formed on his skin.

But this wasn't his wife. This was…a woman who looked very similar to Sande Williams. Blond hair, petite frame. Somewhat rounder face…the lips noticeably thinner.

The gasp next to him shook Patrick from his intense study of the obviously dead victim in the photograph. Sande's horrified gaze was fixed on the image.

"Do you understand now why I needed to bring you in?" Lyons asked.

She nodded slowly. "If that's Sande Williams…" Her gaze collided with Patrick's. "Then who am I?"

"That's a damn good question," Lyons growled.

Patrick jerked his attention to the less than tactful officer. "No more games, Detective. What's going on here?"

Lyons withdrew another photograph from the file and placed it on the table. "This was Nancy Childers, also of D.C."

Like the other photo, the deceased female lay on a stainless steel morgue table with a white sheet covering her body. Physically, the victim was a fairly close match to the Nancy Childers murdered only a few hours ago.

"My question is why we have two pairs of women with the same names and similar physical descriptions." He tapped the first photo, then the second. "Not twins, mind you. Just women who look a hell of a lot alike at first glance."

Sande shook her head slowly, her attention glued to the photos. "I don't understand."

"That makes two of us," Lyons said.

"What gives you reason to believe these two victims are connected?" Patrick gestured to the photographs. Admittedly, there was no way this situation was a mere coincidence, yet stranger things happened. There had to be something else Lyons had opted not to share.

"Both murders were executed using the same M.O. Each victim was involved in an identity theft ring that's currently under investigation."

"In D.C.," Patrick suggested. The detective had said that Sande Williams was suspected of a crime in D.C., not Chicago.

"We've traced that same ring to Chicago and New York. We could be looking at something bigger than that. We just don't know yet." He turned to Sande. "You're the first we've discovered with amnesia."

The detective's closed expression made Patrick's instincts buzz. "You've tracked down other members of this ring?"

Lyons didn't respond right away, but his eyes told Patrick he wasn't going to like his answer.

"Between our investigation and the ongoing one in D.C. we've connected ten suspects."

"Have interviews or interrogations revealed any details that may be useful to my client's situation?" Patrick was swiftly growing impatient with the detective's stall tactics.

"We have zip."

"You've collared ten suspects and you have nothing in the way of information as to how this operation works or the motives behind it?" Maybe if he excavated long and hard enough he'd get half the story out of the man.

"We have zip," Lyons reiterated, "because your client is the first suspect we've connected to this operation who's still alive."

SHE WAS SUPPOSED TO BE dead.

Sande now knew without doubt that when she'd awakened outside that morgue, it had been a mistake.

She wasn't supposed to wake up.

"You don't drink coffee," O'Brien said as he settled on the sofa next to her. "How about tea or…" He shrugged. "Water. If you're a chocolate fan, unfortunately, I'm all out of hot cocoa."

"No, thank you." Sande wasn't thirsty or hungry. She was tired. Tired and frustrated.

"Let's talk about the feelings you experienced when you realized you didn't like coffee." O'Brien reclined against the back of the sofa and settled that dark gaze on her.

No matter how impatient she'd been or how irrational she'd behaved, his patience seemed unwavering. He just kept on being there, prodding her along.

There was something she needed to say before this went any further. "First, I want to thank you for taking me in." The thought of going back to that shelter, as nice as it was, had been more than she could bear. No matter the security on site, right now she trusted no one except O'Brien.

He waved a hand. "No problem. My job is to see that you're safe and secure."

His associate, Windy, had made the same offer when she'd met them at the precinct. But Sande felt safest with O'Brien. Maybe because he was a man. She couldn't say for certain, but something about him made her feel secure, or calm. Both, she decided.

"Still, I appreciate your going above and beyond. I'm sure taking clients home with you isn't in your job description." Especially one who might be crazy.

One of those broad shoulders lifted, then fell nonchalantly. "You're the first, but, as I said, it's not a problem."

She sighed. Time to answer his question about the coffee. "I don't know. There was this heaviness in my stomach. A revulsion almost. I just knew I couldn't drink coffee."

He nodded. "It felt real, instinctive."

"Yes."

"That's progress."

She noticed he didn't say it was a good sign or that it meant she was on her way to regaining her memory. Progress… She supposed that was something.

Time to ask the hard questions. "Why can't I

remember anything? As far as I can tell I haven't suffered any head trauma. You think it's drugs?"

"That's possible." He contemplated her question for what felt like forever. "Your condition could be psychological for reasons other than the involvement of drugs."

He'd mentioned that before. "You mean, I don't want to remember."

"Not necessarily. Though it would appear you've suffered no physical trauma, there may have been extreme emotional trauma."

She stared straight into his eyes. He needed to be completely on the level with her. No skirting the truth, no matter how hard it was to take. "Will I regain my memory?" She bit her lip, then blurted the rest. "Will I get *me* back?"

*Whoever me is.*

That was the thing. If she wasn't Sande Williams, who was she? There was no match on her prints. The Illinois DMV considered her Sande Williams. But the dead Sande Williams in the photo in Lyon's case file had possessed a license from D.C. So the driver's license didn't really mean anything. Unfortunately, getting a driver's license under a name other than your own wasn't so difficult.

"If," O'Brien began, emphasizing the word, "you'd suffered the kind of head trauma necessary to cause global amnesia, the answer would be no. You likely would not ever recall your past."

Sande frowned. "Global amnesia. I'm not sure I understand what that means."

"Complete amnesia. No recall whatsoever." He held up a hand when she would have thrown two more questions at him. "But that's not the case here. Most patients with that level of amnesia have to learn to walk, talk, basically everything, all over again."

That was a relief. Or was it? "So, what if drugs are involved?" She wasn't sure what was scarier, drugs or emotional trauma. Drugs meant someone had introduced pharmaceuticals into her body. But that would clear up eventually, wouldn't it? If she'd experienced some emotional horror, remembering it could be more painful than any damage the drugs may have done.

"A lot would depend upon the drug used." He reached for the final French fry on his plate. They'd picked up takeout on the way to his home. Burgers and fries she had known without doubt she loved.

When he'd finished off the fry, he continued, "There are a number of drugs that cause temporary memory loss. Not usually to this extent or even for this long. But there are dozens of experimental drugs out there that might create this very scenario. There's just no way to know without the lab results. We should have those results tomorrow."

"More waiting." She slipped off her shoes and pulled her knees to her chest.

"More waiting," he confirmed.

Sande chastised herself for not thanking Windy for the clothes; she'd picked up jeans, sweaters, undies, socks and sneakers. Patrick's partner had gone out of her way to be helpful and nice; and Sande owed her for her kindness, as well as the clothes. But after the visit to the precinct, she hadn't been able to think about anything except the pictures of those murder victims.

Was the blond woman the real Sande Williams?

Her pulse rate started to gallop, and she closed her eyes and ordered it to slow. She couldn't keep it together if she allowed her emotions to get out of control. She had to think clearly. Rationally.

Opening her eyes, she decided a subject change was in order. "You know—" she turned to O'Brien "—I think I'll have tea after all."

He pushed himself to his feet. "Sugar?"

Sande considered the question a moment. "Yes. Definitely sugar."

When he'd headed for the kitchen, she got up and walked around the room. The space was large for a condo. She wasn't sure how she knew that but she did. Not a lot of color. Mostly whites and beiges. Probably the place had already been painted when he moved in. In contrast, the furnishings were dark and heavy. Lots of leather and wood. Masculine. Not surprising. O'Brien was definitely a man's man. Probably somewhere in the condo was a weight bench where he worked out. A guy couldn't keep muscles that well defined without working at it.

She'd made her second trip around the room before she realized what was missing. Pictures. There were no personal pictures. There was art—sculpture as well as paintings. But no pictures of family or friends or favorite places.

"Tea for the lady," he announced as he entered the room. No fancy tray, just a steaming mug with the tea label hanging loosely from one side.

Sande took the hot mug into her hands. The heat felt good. "Thanks."

He resumed his seat on one end of the sofa and she settled onto the other end, as before. She tasted the tea. "Mmm. Good. Thanks."

"My pleasure."

She sipped the warm liquid for a while to work up the nerve to delve into the subject gnawing at her. "So tell me about you."

His unguarded expression immediately went into lockdown. "What do you want to know?"

He definitely had secrets. Or just stuff he didn't want to talk about. "Are you originally from Chicago?" Start with the basics.

"I am." He didn't meet her eyes as he answered. Instead, he busied himself cleaning up the remnants of their dinner.

"How long have you worked for the Colby Agency?"

"Two years, two months and one week."

"Ah ha. The move to the agency was a major career change?" Only a significant one would be remembered so precisely.

"It was." He stood, hamburger wrappers and fry bags in hand. "Excuse me."

His reaction to her questions confused her. Made her more curious. Clearly, he didn't want to talk about himself. But when he returned and took his seat once more, he didn't tell her to change the subject, so she kept going.

"What did you do before?"

This time he looked directly at her when he answered. "I was a psychologist."

She blinked to cover her surprise. Wow. She certainly hadn't expected that answer. "As in *Dr.* Patrick O'Brien?"

"Not anymore. I'm just plain Patrick O'Brien now." His face remained impassive.

"Ever been married?" He wore no ring, and considering there wasn't a single picture of a woman in his home, she was pretty sure he wasn't now.

"Once."

"Divorced?"

"No."

A knot formed in her stomach. "Your wife died?" Why, oh why, had she started down this path? No wonder his expression had closed so completely. She was a horrible person. Here he was, being so nice to her, and she had to go and bring up a painful past.

"Yes."

When she would have relayed how sorry she was for his loss, he interrupted. "It was three years ago. She was murdered by the wife of one of her many extramarital conquests."

Dear God. What kind of woman did that to a man like this? "I didn't mean to bring up such a painful subject." Sande set her tea on the end table. "I was being selfish. I didn't want to think about my problems anymore, so I nosed into yours. Sorry."

Those dark eyes held hers. He made no attempt to disguise the sadness or the contempt in them. "It is what it is. I thought I knew her. I was wrong. I won't make that mistake again."

Silence seemed to suck the air out of the room for the next few seconds. His last statement was the saddest one of all. This man, who had trusted and loved, would never allow himself to be hurt again. Or to feel.

*None of your business.*

Definitely. Sande decided the best way to get past it was to ask the next question. "Did the police get her killer?"

He nodded. "The wife and the thug she hired to do the job."

"I'm—"

"Don't say you're sorry again. It's over. There's nothing else to say."

Talk about living in denial. She wondered why a psychologist couldn't see that in himself, when he surely recognized it in patients all the time.

Was she in denial? She assumed she would get her past back. Was she wrong to blindly assume anything? If the people after her had their way, she would end up dead on a stainless steel table just like the other Sande Williams. And both Nancy Childers's.

Back to O'Brien. Talking about him was a lot less stressful for her.

"Have you dated anyone since…recently?"

A glimmer of a smile haunted his lips. "Are you asking about my social life?"

Her cheeks heated. "Yes, I guess I am."

"I'm afraid you'd find it rather boring." He chuckled. "But to answer your question, yes, I have dated from time to time."

That was good. "That's the right attitude." She

hugged her knees to her chest once more. "Being alone stinks."

He seemed to realize at the same instant she did that the statement had come straight from the heart.

"You know loneliness, do you?"

She laughed softly, dryly. "Evidently."

"Sometimes people need solitude to heal."

Spoken like a true shrink. "I don't like being alone."

This time her frank statement startled her. Her chest tightened and her heart rate increased.

"Now we know two things about you," O'Brien offered. "You don't like coffee or being alone."

"That's good, right?"

He smiled. Her breath caught. Patrick O'Brien was a very good-looking man, but when he smiled, he was gorgeous.

"That's progress," he reminded her.

"Progress. Right." For the first time today she felt relaxed. Definitely safe.

"I'm sure you're tired." O'Brien stood. "Why don't I show you to the guest room?"

Yes, she was tired. But she had a feeling that he was also tired. Tired of her questions, perhaps.

"Good idea." She grabbed her shoes and followed him into the hall between the living area and the kitchen.

He stopped at the first door on the left. "Let me

know if you need anything. There's a T-shirt on the bed. I hope that'll work for you to sleep in."

"That's fine. Thank you."

When he would have turned away, Sande did something that startled her all over again.

"Is it possible to lose everything and ever be happy again?"

He turned back to her, searched her eyes. No doubt for the motive behind the question. She realized too late that it probably hit a little too close to home for his comfort. But, in truth, the question was about her.

Or maybe it was about him, too.

"There are varying degrees of happiness, Sande. Don't mistake a lesser degree for unhappiness. Life is what you make it. You work with what you've got." He called good-night over his shoulder as he walked away.

"Night." She watched him disappear into his room. "But what if you don't have anything?" she murmured.

It was hard to work with something you didn't have.

She might not ever remember her real name or the life she'd had before, but somehow, some part of her instinctively sensed that her life—her real life—was pretty damn empty.

## Chapter Seven

Patrick woke to a scream.

He threw back the covers and jumped out of bed.
*Sande.*

He rushed to the guest room, switching on the hall light as he went. She sat in the middle of the bed, sobbing. He settled on the edge of the mattress, facing her, and he gently took her by the shoulders to get her attention.

"You okay?"

She wiped her eyes and nose and lifted her tear-filled gaze to his. "I…was back at the hospital. On the gurney. Only this time I couldn't wake up because…I was dead."

He pulled her into his arms and held her tightly in spite of the alarms going off in his head. This was too personal, too close. But he had to comfort her. "It was just a dream. The photos Detective Lyons showed you probably prompted the nightmare. You're fine."

She drew away. Shook her head. "I'm not fine. I don't know who I am. I don't know anything." She wrenched her arms free of his touch. "Nothing's ever going to be fine again."

The emotional turmoil and desperation were to be expected after a day like today. "The way you feel right now is completely understandable. You have to trust me on that." He mustered up a smile. "Remember, I used to be a psychologist."

Even that didn't stop the quivering of her lips. He shouldn't stare at her full mouth for more than a second, but he did. She had beautiful lips.

"Yeah, yeah. All this crap is understandable." She sniffed. "So can I call you Doc?" That she managed a little smile through the tears still shining in her eyes weakened his defenses.

"Sure. Why not? I've been called worse."

This time she laughed out loud. The sound was a little shaky, but a whole lot sweet. It was the first time he'd heard her laugh. He liked the way it sounded. Liked the way her whole face lit up.

"I can't believe you don't have hot cocoa, Doc." She pushed the hair back from her face. "It's practically winter. Everybody stocks cocoa when it gets cold. Don't you know that?"

"I take it you're a chocolate fan as well." That she was recognizing more and more of her likes and dislikes was hopeful.

"It would seem so." She took a deep, uneven breath. "I guess more tea would be okay."

"Come on." He stood, offered his hand. "We'll see what we can dig up."

She placed her palm in his and his heart reacted. The response stunned Patrick. He hadn't felt that particular squeezing sensation of excitement in…years. He shouldn't now, but he couldn't let go. She needed his touch.

When they discovered a box of instant hot cocoa mix he didn't remember buying, his client was exceedingly pleased. A little boiling water and they were in business.

"This is heaven," she insisted as she held the cup of hot cocoa and breathed in its sweet smell.

"Enjoy." He pulled a chair from the kitchen table and waited for her to sit.

"Thank you." She eased into the chair, careful not to spill her cocoa.

He dropped into the chair next to her, his attention abruptly wandering to her state of dress. She was wearing his T-shirt. No jeans covered her toned legs.

Quite shortsighted of him not to consider that would happen when he'd offered the T-shirt. His body tightened irrationally. It hadn't been that long since he'd been this close to a half-naked woman. The whole protector thing was obviously playing havoc with his logic.

He cleared his mind and focused back on business. "Tell me about your dream." Often dreams were gateways to one's innermost thoughts and fears. Maybe he could glean additional insight from her.

"I was back in the hospital. I couldn't move or speak or even open my eyes." She shuddered. "It was horrible."

"Think carefully." He cradled his cup of cocoa, let the heat erase the feel of her skin from his palm. "The smallest detail could be significant."

She sat very still for long enough to make him rethink his question. If her condition were unstable, she had displayed no symptoms so far. He needed to prod her, but not push too hard. It was a delicate balance. One he hadn't practiced in almost three years.

"There was someone speaking to me." Lines of concentration marked her brow as she chewed on her bottom lip. "A man, I think."

Patrick shifted in his chair, uncomfortable with where his thoughts detoured when she did that. She was a client. A client with a major issue. He had to keep his thoughts in line. Strange, he hadn't experienced this problem before in his career at the Colby

Agency. But he understood it for what it was. The need to protect. To win. He'd failed his wife and himself. Some part of him subconsciously wanted to ensure he didn't fail this time. This woman.

"Can you recall anything he said?"

"Something about termination." She shook her head. "I'm not sure."

"That's okay. Whatever you can recall is all that matters." Despite his reassurance, he felt perched on the edge of discovery. He wanted her to remember more.

"Wait." She sat up straighter. "There was a woman."

Anticipation fired in his veins. "Did she speak?"

Sande shook her head slowly. "I don't… No. Wait. She did. She argued with the man. I couldn't make out her words, but she didn't agree with his decision."

Had Sande been a part of an experiment scheduled for termination? The concept was a bit sci-fi, but not totally outside the realm of feasibility. There were unscrupulous scientists out there who would try most anything given the funding and opportunity.

Patrick's cell phone vibrated. "Keep going over the details." He withdrew the phone from his pocket. "I should take this call."

He frowned. Almost 1:00 a.m. He checked the screen. Not Windy. Unknown caller. "O'Brien."

"Mr. O'Brien, this is Alma Spears. I know it's the middle of the night but I need to talk to you."

Patrick's senses moved to a new level of alert. "How can I help you?" He didn't call her by name so as not to distract Sande.

"I'm sorry to phone so late, but something strange happened here tonight and I thought you might want to know."

More of that fierce tension rippled through his body. "I'm listening."

"I think Sande is in real danger. One of those men called and insisted I tell him where she was. I kept telling him I didn't know, but I don't think he believed me."

"When was this?" Patrick was out of his chair before the order to stand had formed in his brain.

"About half an hour ago." She fell silent for several seconds. "I don't know how to say this, but I feel like he might have been threatening me."

"Is there someone you could stay with tonight?" Patrick immediately considered calling Detective Lyons to request protection for the woman.

"No, there's no place to go. I'm on my own." She sighed. "Maybe I'm overreacting. It was just such an uncomfortable conversation."

"I'm coming over." The decision was made and spoken in the same instant. His gaze settled on Sande. He would have no choice but to take her along. No way was he allowing her out of his sight.

"Stay put, and don't let anyone in. We'll be there in twenty minutes."

Ms. Spears assured him she would do as he instructed, and he ended the call. "Get dressed." He put his cup in the sink and headed for his room to dress as well, without waiting for Sande's response.

"What's going on? Was that Windy?" Her voice followed him down the hall.

"No." He paused long enough to look back at her. "That was Alma Spears. She needs to talk to me. We're going over there. We need to hurry."

It wasn't until that moment that he considered he'd been talking to Sande all this time while wearing nothing but a pair of sweatpants. She wasn't the only one who'd been sitting around that table half-dressed. He should have pulled on a T-shirt. Where was his sense of professionalism? Missing in action, obviously.

By the time he'd dressed and grabbed his coat from the closet, Sande was ready as well.

"Can you tell me what she said?"

"On the way."

He didn't want to waste any time. En route, he put in a call to Windy. He wasn't about to jump into a situation, putting his client at risk, without backup. For all he knew, someone could have forced Ms. Spears to make that call. On second thought, he called Detective Lyons, too. Might as well go in prepared.

As they rolled down the dark, quiet street where Ms. Spears lived, Sande abruptly grasped the armrest. "I can't go back there."

Patrick braked. Windy wasn't here yet. He should hold off on pulling into the driveway until either she or Lyons was on hand.

"What's wrong?" He shifted his full attention to the woman seated next to him. Her agitation was palpable. The tension vibrating in her small frame set him on edge.

"This is where they picked me up." She turned her face to his. "They were supposed to terminate me. But they didn't. They made a mistake or something."

Patrick put the vehicle in Park and surveyed the street. Deserted. No vehicles other than the ones under carports. "Did you experience this in the dream?"

She moved her head from side to side in a slow, hypnotic manner. "I just know." She pointed to the house where Nancy Childers had been murdered. "I was there. They came for me. I tried to run, but they caught me."

Patrick scrubbed a hand over his chin. New warnings were going off in his head. He should drive away. Wait down the block for Lyons or Windy.

The question was settled when Windy's car pulled up next to his. "You want to go to the door now or wait for Lyons?" she asked as soon as they'd lowered their windows. But then the detective roared up the street, parked nose to nose with Patrick.

Patrick glanced at his partner. "Impeccable timing."

She rolled her eyes, obviously not caring for the cop's condescending attitude any more than he did.

Before opening his door, Patrick said to Sande, "Stay close to me."

She nodded.

"What the devil is going on?" Lyons demanded as he approached the sidewalk where Patrick waited.

"Exactly what I told you on the phone." He gestured to Alma Spears's home. "She called. I responded."

The detective didn't look convinced, but he didn't argue. "Well, let's check it out."

As instructed, Sande stuck close to Patrick's side as the four of them crossed the street to the house. Patrick rapped on the door. "Ms. Spears, it's Patrick O'Brien."

No response.

Lyons tipped his head. "See if it's locked."

Patrick didn't hesitate. He wrapped his fingers around the knob and gave it a twist. The door opened. Beside him, Sande shivered.

Nancy Childers's door had been ajar when her body was discovered. Did this mean…

"Step aside," Lyons ordered as he withdrew his service weapon.

Patrick was glad to do so. He kept Sande close behind him and followed the detective inside. Windy brought up the rear.

"Ms. Spears!" Lyons called out. "This is Detective Lyons. If you're hiding, you can come out. You're safe now."

Silence echoed in the house. The living room and adjoining dining room were as deserted as the street outside.

"I'll take the kitchen," Windy said, not waiting for the detective's authorization.

"I've got the upstairs," Patrick announced.

"Garage," Lyons barked, not about to be outdone.

"Stay behind me," Patrick murmured to Sande as they approached the narrow staircase.

She nodded and moved in close behind him once more.

Slowly, listening intently for the slightest sound, Patrick climbed the stairs. On the second-story landing, he flipped a switch to flood the corridor with light. Four doors. The first was a bedroom. Next a bathroom. Still no sign of the resident.

"Wait." Sande grasped his arm. "I don't think I can do this."

Patrick nodded. "Let me take you back down to stay with Windy."

For several deafeningly quiet seconds Sande stood

frozen, uncertain what to do. Then she shook her head. "No. I'm going with you."

"You're sure?" Although he doubted that any intruder would hang around after they'd entered the house, he couldn't be certain.

She nodded, crept closer to him.

"Okay."

The next door was to another bedroom that obviously served as a sewing room.

As Patrick moved toward the final door, adrenaline rushed through him. Every instinct warned that trouble waited behind it.

He reached out, grasped the knob, then opened the door. Darkness greeted them, as it had in the other rooms. He flipped the switch and light flooded the space.

The initial image his brain assimilated was Alma Spears lying peacefully on her bed. Her arms were at her sides, her eyes closed. On first glance she appeared to be sleeping. But after a moment or two her chest wasn't rising and falling with the intake and release of air.

She wasn't breathing.

He rushed to the bed, felt her carotid artery. No pulse. But her skin was still warm.

"Have Lyons call 9-1-1."

Sande rushed from the room. Patrick assumed the necessary position for performing CPR.

By the time Sande returned, he knew he was getting nowhere fast. Windy elbowed him aside. "Let me take over."

Patrick didn't resist.

He watched as his partner delivered the life-giving puffs of breath, then repeated the chest compressions.

Wouldn't matter.

Alma Spears was dead.

Lyons rushed into the room. "Paramedics are on their way." He moved in next to Windy, tried to help.

"It was supposed to be me," Sande murmured.

Patrick turned to her, and her gaze met his. "I didn't need a nightmare to tell me." Her attention settled on the bed once more. "I'm supposed to be dead."

Patrick's arm was around her shoulders before his brain could warn that the maneuver might not be such a good idea. "I told you I wouldn't let anything happen to you and I won't. You have to trust me."

Her eyes searched his. "There are two things I know for sure. That I do trust you." Her gaze flicked back to the unmoving body of the older woman. "And that I'm supposed to be dead."

When Patrick would have protested, she put her hands over her ears, then held them palms out to silence him.

"You don't understand. I *am* supposed to be dead. I know that with every fiber of my being." Sande took a step back, physically distancing herself from Patrick. "And until I'm dead, anyone who gets in the way will die."

# Chapter Eight

Alma Spears had been suffocated with her own pillow. A definite deviation from the M.O. of the other murders related to Detective Lyons's case.

It was five o'clock Saturday morning before Patrick was able to bring Sande back to his house. Lyons had insisted that they hang around until the neighbors were interviewed and the coroner had taken the body away.

The detective was convinced that Ms. Spears was not involved in the identity theft operation, but was perhaps suspected of knowing too much just because she was a nosy neighbor. Patrick had reached the same conclusion, though he wasn't ruling out anything just yet. He had learned the hard way that even the most innocuous situation could in reality be devastation in disguise.

Patrick peeked into the guest room to ensure

Sande was finally asleep. He could use more coffee. Sleep was out of the question for him. During their initial interview Lyons had given him ten minutes to review first-hand the file so far amassed on the case. His captain wouldn't be happy if he discovered that one of his detectives had provided too much information to an outsider regarding an ongoing investigation. To give an overview was one thing, but to allow Patrick to flip through the reports was entirely another. But Lyons had taken the risk. His motive was easily discernible. Lyons wanted to solve the case. Whatever it took.

There were details in the case file that didn't compute for Patrick. Lyons himself confessed to being baffled by the strange directions the sparse evidence and reports accumulated indicated. Which was probably the only reason Lyons had allowed Patrick access to the file.

Ten victims, excluding Alma Spears. Three cities, D.C., Chicago and New York. Ten murders, all with the same M.O., again excluding Alma. Each victim used a stolen identity; the Sande Williams and Nancy Childers identity appeared to have been stolen twice.

*If that's Sande Williams...then who am I?*

That was the question of the hour. Sande had asked for help from the Colby Agency nearly forty-eight hours ago, and they were no closer to discovering her past or the reason she'd awakened at the morgue than they had been then.

Not a single hit had come back on her prints. No one had reported her missing. Other than the driver's license and social security number, there was absolutely nothing that connected her to this planet.

But no one came into the world fully grown. Prior to forty-eight hours ago this woman existed somewhere, somehow. Finding out how and where might be impossible, however, if significant portions of her memory did not return. The drug screen results would be back later today or early tomorrow. Patrick was hoping those results would provide an answer. If drugs were involved, reconstructing Sande's past successfully would depend entirely on the cellular damage left behind.

If drugs weren't involved, then he would have to assume that her reasons for not remembering were related to psychological trauma. Exposing her to places where she had reportedly been before may or may not have prodded the few memories that had surfaced thus far. The dream, as well, could be relevant, but just as easily not. The brain still held many mysteries, not the least of which was memory. In recent years much had been learned about how activities and thoughts were stored in one's cells. And yet there was so very, very much more to learn.

That Sande had the same name as a murder victim suspected of having stolen identities could be coincidence, but not likely. Still, if the victims were related, there had to be a connection.

His client as well as Nancy Childers had supposedly worked at Peyton and Wyatt, a corporate accounting firm that provided consulting analysis as well as accounting support for large corporations. Where had the other victims been employed? Could that be the connection?

Patrick put a call through on his cell to Lyons. He felt confident the detective was still in his office. Like Patrick, he wouldn't be getting much sleep until this puzzle was solved.

When Lyons answered on the second ring, Patrick knew he'd guessed right. The detective sounded tired and flustered, especially when he learned who was calling.

"One question," Patrick pressed, despite Lyons's insistence that he had a meeting in two minutes. "Where were the other victims employed?"

Patrick wrote down the names as Lyons reviewed the file and called off each one. The Nancy Childers and Sande Williams of Chicago were the only ones to be employed at the same firm.

After thanking the detective Patrick tossed his cell phone aside. He studied the names of companies and firms. Nine in total. According to Lyons, three of the companies were aerospace contractors, two specialized in electronics technology, two others were pharmaceutical and medical research companies, respectively, while the final two were accounting firms, one being Peyton and Wyatt. A varied range of businesses with no ready way to connect one to the other.

Patrick dropped his pen and exhaled a frustrated breath. Not exactly what he'd hoped for. And yet there could be a connecting thread. It wasn't completely out of the realm of possibility.

All he had to do was find it.

SANDE WOKE SUDDENLY.

Her heart raced and her skin felt damp with sweat.

More nightmares. Struggling to calm her emotions, she reminded herself that she was safe. With O'Brien. He would protect her.

Sitting upright, she pulled her knees to her chest and rested her head there. When her breathing had returned to normal she forced herself to analyze the dreams. A medical or research lab. Definitely a lab or hospital of some sort. In the dream she was a patient. She could hear voices discussing her, but she couldn't see any faces. Her eyes had refused to open.

Was her dream about the hospital where she'd awakened on that gurney outside the morgue? Or was this someplace else?

She should tell O'Brien about her dream. It had to mean something, otherwise the same one wouldn't keep haunting her. She wiggled free of the covers and went in search of her host. If he was sleeping, she would just have to nose around in the kitchen for more hot cocoa and wait him out. She doubted he'd gotten much rest last night. He was likely as exhausted as she was.

After peeking into the other rooms along the hall, she confirmed that O'Brien had done exactly what she'd figured he would: he'd stayed up. Foolishly, it made her heart glad that someone cared enough to miss sleep on her account. But then, that was his job. He was investigating her case, protecting his client. It wasn't as if he worried about her on a personal level.

A pang of sadness settled deep in her chest. Maybe that was the worst part of all. Not having anyone who really cared whether she lived or died. No one should be that alone.

She found O'Brien working on a laptop in his kitchen. The smell of coffee brewing filled the air.

O'Brien looked up as she entered the room. He'd pulled back on the same navy slacks and pin-striped shirt he'd had on yesterday. Only the tie and jacket were missing.

"Tea?" he offered as she neared the table where he worked. "I made coffee, but I put on the kettle as well just in case you wanted tea or cocoa."

She nodded. Tea would work. "I'll get it."

"Mugs are in the cabinet above the coffeemaker."

"I had more of those weird dreams." She poured herself a steaming mug of hot water and dunked in the teabag he'd set out for her, then added a little sugar. She joined him at the table. "Basically the same dream, just a bit more vivid."

He studied her a moment. "Give me the new details."

She sipped her tea and mentally reviewed both dreams. "I was definitely in some sort of lab or hospital. The voices had the same conversation about whether I was to be terminated or not. One distinctly male, the other female." She shrugged. "That's about it."

"I've found what I think may be a connection between the victims. A very loose one, mind you, but I believe it's a link nonetheless." He closed the laptop and refilled his mug before continuing.

Anticipation had Sande gripping her own mug with both hands. "What kind of connection?"

When he'd lowered his tall frame into his chair once more, he settled his full attention on her. "Each of the ten victims worked at a company where technology, research or corporate accounting was the focus. In each case, the victim had been employed there less than one year. And—" he held up a hand for emphasis "—each stolen identity used to get the position with the company was one with the necessary credentials."

Though she was following what he was saying, "What about the people whose identities were used."

"Not one had any idea her or his identity was being illegally used until after the murder."

"Except, if there is another Sande Williams or Nancy Childers out there, they haven't been found yet." The thought left Sande feeling empty and cold despite the heat from the tea. If she wasn't Sande Williams, who was she? How long would it take to find that answer?

"Exactly."

She downed a couple more gulps of tea, hoping the caffeine would make her feel human again. "So, you think these identities were stolen for a particular reason—their business credentials?"

"Yes. Which ultimately means the stolen identities weren't the targets, they were merely tools to reach the true targets."

"The companies?" The whole idea was starting to feel surreal. Why would anyone steal someone else's identify to get a job?

"Information," O'Brien explained. "Maybe technology or research data. But definitely information.

The people utilizing these stolen identities could have been spies or moles, placed in certain key positions to gather the information needed." He flared his hands. "Or to contaminate that information if hired by a competing company or firm."

The mug suddenly felt too heavy to hold. Sande placed it on the table in front of her, her mind churning with the ugliness of what or who she might turn out to be. "That would make me a thief." She moistened her lips. "A bad person." A knot formed in her stomach.

"Don't go there." O'Brien reached across the table and placed a hand on her arm. She wanted to draw away, but there was such warmth in his touch, such strength, she couldn't bear to do so. "It's very possible that considering the circumstances, your amnesia and the fact that you're clearly on the run, you were an unwilling participant."

Relief trickled through her. "That makes me feel a little better." She did not want to be a criminal. It would really suck to regain her memory and realize she was a thief, or worse.

A killer.

She shuddered.

But that was a real possibility. The truth was she had no idea who she was or what she had done in her life.

Anything was possible.

The cell phone lying on the table vibrated. Sande jumped. She stared at the phone, somewhere in the back of her mind realizing it was past 9:00 a.m. The call could be about the test results.

Or news about who she really was.

"O'Brien."

Her body trembled in spite of her determination to be strong. Whatever she had done, whoever she was, she would simply have to face the consequences.

O'Brien's responses were limited to "okay" and "I understand." Sande found herself holding her breath when he disconnected.

"The test results are in."

His tone sent the last of the warmth draining right out of her. "And?"

He shook his head. "Nothing."

Somehow she had hoped the answer would be that simple—that she'd been drugged. When the effects wore off completely she would remember everything and all would be right in her world once more. That would somehow prove she was a victim, not a criminal.

"Oh." Defeat sucked at her resolve.

"There were some inconsistencies the lab couldn't explain…" He hesitated. "But that doesn't mean anything significant. It just means there may have been something there that is no longer detectable…at least without us knowing to look specifically for whatever it was."

Hope welled once more. "So I *could* have been drugged or something?"

"There's still that possibility."

He didn't sound very convinced, but at this point she would take whatever hope he offered, however vague or remote.

"What do we do now?"

Sitting here waiting for the other shoe to drop was not exactly what she hoped he had on the agenda for today. She needed to do something besides wait for the bad guys to figure out where she was.

*Bad guys.* Were the men who'd chased her at the hospital and then again on the street her former associates? Was she one of them? God, she hoped that wasn't the case.

O'Brien stood. "We're going to see Detective Lyons. I want to run my theories by him." He pushed in his chair. "In person."

Sande experienced another of those chills as she attempted to read between the lines of what he'd just said. "Are you concerned that someone might be listening in on your telephone conversations?" Could the bad guys have already figured out where she was? Were they watching right now?

"No." He put his coffee mug in the sink. "I want

to see the detective's face when I ask him why he hasn't already considered this scenario. Or if he has, why he didn't share that theory with me."

"You think Lyons might be involved with *them?*"

O'Brien took the mug from her hand and placed it in the sink. "I'm exploring all possibilities."

She caught herself chewing on her lip, and stopped. No need to let him see just how worried she was. "Good idea."

"First," he qualified, "I need a shower."

She could use one, as well. "Another good idea."

O'Brien showed her to the guest bathroom and rounded up the bag Windy had given her. There were toiletries and more clothes inside.

"I'll be right down the hall." He paused. "I'll leave the door open. Yell if you need me."

For a split second before he turned away their gazes met, and Sande felt a distinctly sexual intensity. Only when he walked away was she able to breathe again.

The heat that had filled her body in that brief moment made her feel more alive…more real.

How long had it been since anyone had looked at her that way? Since she'd felt any sort of connection to another human?

Was there someone out there with whom she'd been involved? Someone who loved her?

No. Probably not.

Anyone who loved her would be looking for her. Wouldn't they?

So far the only people searching for her seemed to be ones who wanted to hurt her. Or take her back to that gurney and stick another tag on her toe.

She turned on the water in the shower and slowly stripped off her clothes. If a person was supposed to die, what happened if he or she somehow avoided that fate? Would destiny catch up and ensure that course played out in the end?

Could a person really cheat fate?

Sande had no idea if she was a spiritual person or not, but just then praying felt like the right thing to do. She stepped beneath the spray of hot water and she prayed. Prayed for God to help her find the truth and for him to forgive her for whatever wrong things she might have done in the past.

Bracing against the cool tile wall, she let the emotions spill from her. Better now than later, when O'Brien would see. She wanted him to believe she was brave and strong. When, in truth, she was neither. She was terrified.

Scolding herself, she forced the fears back down to a more tolerable level. The only thing stopping her from being brave and strong was her own self-doubt.

No matter who she had been or what she had done

in the past, God evidently had plans for her. Otherwise he would never have sent her to the Colby Agency and her own personal guardian angel.

Sande thought of Madge, the homeless lady who lived in a cardboard condo, but had taken her in, put clothes on her naked body and taken her to find help.

The Colby Agency.

# Chapter Nine

Patrick stood at the precinct's duty desk and waited patiently. It was 8:00 a.m. and Detective Lyons couldn't be found. He'd left for a meeting and hadn't returned or called in.

The duty officer hung up the phone and shook her head. "He's still not answering his cell."

"And you have no idea where this meeting was or who he planned to meet?"

The young sergeant shook her head again. "Sorry. No. He didn't say." She shrugged. "But that's not unusual. Lyons does things his way. He could be gone for hours." She surveyed her desk once more, then met Patrick's eyes. "Half the time his partner doesn't even know his schedule."

Lyons hadn't mentioned working with anyone on this case, but it made sense that his partner would be up to speed to some extent. "Is his partner in?"

"I'll check." The sergeant picked up the phone once more.

Patrick turned to Sande who hovered close behind him. He doubted she'd gotten any more sleep than he had. She hadn't said much since they'd left his place. He hoped her silence was related to the case and not to his temporary lapse in sanity.

He'd felt it. No doubt she'd seen it. *Need.* Pure. Primal. Right there at the bathroom door. The idea of her taking off her clothes and stepping into the shower had abruptly consumed him. The desire to climb into that shower with her had been fierce.

Not once in three years had he felt the compulsion for sex. Nor had he been attracted to any woman with whom he'd worked, or encountered outside work. He'd assumed that component of his life was over, beyond the occasional date. The part of his brain that reasoned, using his formal training, understood that it would take time for him to get over the loss of his wife, physically and emotionally. His wife, the woman he'd loved and the woman he'd come to hate after learning of her deceit.

But his less rational side had opted not to allow that kind of pain again. The only way to avoid it was to minimize contact with another human on that level.

He'd been successful until now.

That the human he'd allowed to get under his skin

was one whose past was missing in action was, he well knew, his mind's twisted way of reenacting his own past. If he could save Sande Williams, turn her life around, make things right for her, then he would have accomplished what he'd failed with his wife.

All the education, experience and wisdom in the world wouldn't prevent his psyche from attempting to heal itself with a similar deed executed without failure.

Too bad it was the one sure way to take him right back down the most agonizing path of his life.

"You hanging in there?" Dumb question, but it was the best he could do at the moment.

She hugged her arms around her middle and managed a vague nod. "Sure."

He was thankful she didn't ask about the missing detective. Patrick's instincts were humming with the suspicion that Lyons was not simply away at a meeting. Something was wrong.

"Detective Cates'll be right out," the sergeant announced, dragging Patrick's attention back to her.

"Thank you."

Patrick ushered Sande to the short row of seats against the wall on the other side of the precinct's small lobby. "As soon as we talk to Lyons we'll drop by my office and have research start working on a couple of theories I've put together." He'd dealt with the Colby Agency's research department for two years. The people there knew how to dissect a theory and follow through on the smallest element. He could definitely use their help on this one.

Windy was following up on Alma Spears. Any next of kin. Former work associates. Anything that might lead them to someone the woman associated with. Patrick had gotten the impression the lady liked to talk. He seriously doubted her ability to keep secrets. She would have shared whatever was going on in her life. The only question was with whom.

"Mr. O'Brien?"

Patrick faced the man approaching. "Detective Cates?"

"That's right." Cates extended his arm. "I'm Carl Lyons's partner."

Patrick shook hands, then gestured to Sande. "This is Ms. Williams. Can we talk in your office?" Though the lobby was empty at the moment except for the sergeant at the duty desk, officers and detectives walked in and out regularly.

"Sure." Cates gestured to the corridor on the left. "This way."

Once in the cramped office Cates shared with Lyons, Patrick waited for Sande to take a seat before settling into one of his own. He didn't waste time with pleasantries. "Are you working with Detective Lyons on the case involving Ms. Williams?"

Cates shook his head. "Nope. Carl's working on that one with some Bureau hotshot."

The FBI? "He didn't mention that," Patrick stated, making no attempt to conceal his surprise.

The detective spread his arms magnanimously. "He's keeping a tight lid on this one. Supposed to be some big-deal secret." Cates cocked his head and stared directly at Patrick with something that looked far too much like accusation. "But it appears he shared information with you."

Patrick recognized the man's hackles were up on the issue. "Not really. What little he shared had more to do with determining the background of my client than anything else."

Cates glanced at Sande. "What is your client's background?"

Now the detective was fishing. "That's what we're attempting to discover."

"All I can tell you," Cates said as he leaned forward and shuffled through the messages on his desk, "is that I'm out of the loop on this one. Lyons is working with the Bureau and that's that."

No point wasting time if the detective didn't have anything. Patrick rose from his chair, as did Sande. "I appreciate your help, Detective Cates."

"I'll let Carl know you stopped by," he said without looking up.

"Thank you." Patrick ushered Sande out of the office and along the corridor. He didn't slow down or speak until they were outside and in his car.

Before he could say what was on his mind, Sande spoke up. "I don't think that detective is too happy with his partner right now."

"There's definitely an element of discontent." Patrick fished out his cell phone and put in a call to Windy. "Hey, check with the agency's Bureau contact and see if we can learn who's working with Detective Lyons on this stolen identities case. According to his partner, Lyons is definitely working with the Bureau."

Windy assured Patrick she would get right on it.

He tucked his phone back into his pocket. It wasn't that he found it surprising the Bureau was working on this case. What was unusual was that he hadn't heard from whoever was doing so. And that Lyons hadn't mentioned the situation fell under federal jurisdiction. If his Bureau contact had been at the scene of the Childers murder, Lyons hadn't said so. Even more unusual, the agent hadn't wanted in on the interview of Sande Williams.

It wasn't like the Bureau and the Colby Agency were strangers.

"That means it's a bigger case than we first thought," Sande commented.

Patrick met her worried gaze as he braked at an

intersection. "That's likely." He didn't want to say more than was necessary. There was no need to fuel her uncertainty until he had reason. And no choice. That was already occurring far more swiftly than he would like.

His cell phone vibrated. If Windy was getting back to him with word on the Bureau, that was damned fast, even for her. "O'Brien."

"We need to talk."

Lyons.

"Where are you?" Patrick analyzed the man's tone. He sounded distressed.

Patrick's first instinct was to ask why he hadn't mentioned the Bureau but decided to save that for when they were face-to-face.

"Meet me at the coffee shop on the corner of Broadway and Briar Place. There's…"

Patrick waited out the man's silence.

"There's something you need to know about your client."

"I'm on my way." He closed his phone and placed it on the console.

"What's wrong?"

Obviously he hadn't done such a good job of concealing his concern. "That was Lyons. He wants to talk." Patrick shot Sande a reassuring glance. "Maybe we'll get the full story this time."

SATURDAY MORNING SHOPPERS slowed their progress. A full fifteen minutes were required to reach their destination. Then another several to find parking. City life. It could be problematic at times.

Just as Patrick put the car in Park his cell vibrated again. Windy. He listened to the news, his uneasiness mounting, then thanked her before he broke the connection.

Sande watched him, unblinking. She apparently sensed that the news he'd received was not helpful.

"The Bureau isn't involved in this case," he told her. He lifted an eyebrow to emphasize his next point. "At least, not that they're willing to admit." The Colby Agency's contact at the FBI was solid. If he believed the Bureau wasn't involved, then, officially, it wasn't. At least not from the Chicago office. Generally, if another field office followed an investigation out of their own jurisdiction, word was passed along. Cooperation sought through the proper chain of command.

The worry in Sande's eyes deepened. "But why would Lyons lie about that? It doesn't make sense."

"That—" Patrick shut off the engine "—is what we're going to find out."

He and Sande emerged from the car at the same time and walked together across the street. He scanned other vehicles closely to ensure they weren't being watched. He'd kept an eye out for a tail since leaving his condo. That whoever had been following them the day before had suddenly vanished was too much to hope for. Someone was out there watching, waiting for the right opportunity. Patrick had to make sure he didn't give them one.

He had to be ready for their next strike. Considering Alma Spears's death, this case had elevated to a more dangerous level. He couldn't take any unnecessary risks.

The bell on the door jingled as they entered the coffee shop. Patrick scanned the customers' faces, as well as those of the employees. Lyons was not among them. Patrick ordered a coffee and a hot cocoa so as not to draw attention as they waited.

"We'll give him a few minutes." He moved toward a table near the windows. "If Lyons doesn't show, I'll call and find out why." Assuming the detective started answering his cell.

Sande accepted the cocoa and took a seat in one of the chairs. Her appetite was still missing, but the warmth felt good to her hands. O'Brien sat down across from her with his back against the wall. He repeatedly scanned the coffee shop and the entryway. Sande glanced over her shoulder regularly. There was something unnerving about sitting with her back to the door. Anyone could just walk in and fire that single shot into the back of her head.

And then she'd be dead like all the others.

She shivered.

No matter that she couldn't remember who she was or where she'd come from, she didn't want to die.

Not anytime soon, anyway.

When she'd tolerated all the silence she could take, she asked, "Do you think those men are still following us?" They could be keeping a low profile, staying back and watching from a distance. Another of those icy shivers rippled through her insides. If she only knew what she was up against, or what she had done to have these people out to get her.

"Possibly." O'Brien gave another long, slow perusal of the folks milling about in the coffee shop. "I haven't picked up on a tail as of yet, but if they're good enough they could avoid detection."

She thought about the man she'd seen behind the wheel of the car that had chased them. Dark hair. Sunglasses. He'd worn a jacket of some sort. From what she had seen he'd appeared well dressed. But then, what did she expect? For her would-be killer to be dressed like a thug? Wearing a ski mask?

Maybe talking wasn't such a good idea. Every time she asked a question she learned something else she really didn't want to know.

By the time she'd finished her cocoa, O'Brien was growing visibly impatient.

"I guess he's not going to show," she commented with another glance over her shoulder.

"He may have been unavoidably detained, or diverted to a crime scene." Even as he said the words O'Brien scrutinized the comings and goings behind her.

"Do you still believe Detective Lyons knows more than he's telling us?" She was pretty sure of the answer to that one, but asked just to be making conversation, since not talking gave her too much time to think about all the things she didn't know. Not to mention piece together far too many ugly scenarios that might explain who she was and what she'd done in the past.

"Absolutely."

A dark sedan easing up to the curb outside the coffee shop tugged her attention to the window. The driver was the sole occupant. O'Brien was explaining how he would get the truth out of Lyons, whatever he was hiding, that she needn't worry. But Sande didn't respond to his assurances; she was too busy watching the man in the car. As he opened the door and emerged from the vehicle, the hair on the back of her neck stood on end.

The man wore a charcoal suit and dark glasses. He strode confidently into the coffee shop. Sande twisted in her chair to watch him at the counter, where he placed his order. The waitress smiled as if he'd said something charming, and accepted his money. Sande studied his profile. The curve of jaw, the angle of his nose. Coal-black hair cut short. Medium height and build.

Her heart pounded. Drawing in a deep breath felt impossible. What was it about this man that made her react so fiercely?

Cup in hand, he pivoted. He paused halfway, as if looking directly at Sande, but his eyes were hidden by the sunglasses. Then he walked out of the coffee shop and strolled to his car.

Sande started to speak, but then the man opened the driver's side door. He looked right at her again for another of those pulse-pounding seconds. It wasn't until he looked away and lowered himself behind the wheel that her breath left her lungs entirely.

She knew that man.

"I know him."

"What?"

"The man driving off." Sande pointed to the car pulling away from the curb. "I know that man."

O'Brien was on his feet and out the door before she realized he'd moved.

She exited the coffee shop to stand next to him on the sidewalk. O'Brien's fingers were working frantically to enter numbers into his cell phone.

Before she could ask if he was calling Windy or the police, he said, "Got it."

She blinked. "Got what?"

"The license plate number." He surveyed the street and sidewalk in both directions. "Let's go back inside and call this in to Windy. Then—" his gaze met hers "—we'll call Lyons and find out what's keeping him."

They had no sooner returned to their table than another vehicle parked in the very spot the man in the dark glasses had used.

Not the same car, Sande assured herself. Not the car from the chase, either. This one was…

Detective Cates got out of the vehicle and strode toward the coffee shop.

O'Brien finished his call to Windy and closed his phone. "This can't be good."

Sande twisted again to watch the detective enter the coffee shop. He glanced around, spotted them and headed for their table.

"Patrick O'Brien," Cates said, then turned to Sande, "Sande Williams, you're to come with me."

"What's going on, Cates?" O'Brien asked as he rose from his chair. "We're waiting for Detective Lyons to arrive. He wanted us to meet him here."

"We'll talk at the precinct."

A muscle in the detective's jaw flexed rhythmically. It wasn't until then that Sande noticed the hard expression he wore. Whatever was going on, Detective Cates was not happy about it.

"But what about Detective Lyons?" she asked as she pushed back her chair and got to her feet. She still felt a little rattled by the man in the charcoal suit. She knew him. She was certain of it.

"Let's not do this here," Cates insisted.

His eyes burned with fury and another emotion Sande couldn't quite label. Regret, maybe.

"I don't understand," she argued. Maybe she was disoriented from last night's dreams, and then the strange fixation she'd experienced when the stranger appeared in the coffee shop. Whatever the case, she couldn't quite gather her wits.

"Outside," Cates growled. He did an about-face and stormed from the shop.

"Come on." O'Brien placed a reassuring hand on Sande's back. "We should probably do as Detective Cates suggests."

Sande acquiesced. She trusted O'Brien's judgment.

The wind whipped through her hair and stung her cheeks as she joined O'Brien and the detective next to his car. She shivered. It hadn't seemed so cold when they'd arrived. Maybe she just hadn't noticed. What day was it? October 31, or was it November 1 already? Saturday. Not Sunday she was certain.

She'd lost all track of time.

If it was October 31, that meant today was Halloween. Fitting, considering the bizarre turn her life had taken recently.

"Why don't you tell us what's going on, Detective," O'Brien insisted. "Your partner is—"

"Dead."

Sande's heart missed a beat. *Dead?*

"Wait," she blurted, surprised that the word came from her. "He called just—"

"That's why you two are coming with me." Cates looked from Sande to O'Brien. "According to his cell phone, you were the last person he contacted before someone put a bullet in his brain." Cates turned his attention back to Sande. "Just like Alma Spears, even if her manner of death was different. Dead is dead."

"But," O'Brien argued, "*he* called *me.*"

"If the statements you gave at the scene are correct, so did Alma Spears," Cates retorted. "Seems to me death is following you two around." That furious gaze homed in on Sande once more. "I want to know why."

She had been right last night. It seemed anyone who got too close ended up dead.

Instead of her.

# Chapter Ten

"That was Windy." Patrick closed his cell phone and slid it into his jacket pocket.

Sande's eyes widened in anticipation. "Did she learn anything from the license plate?"

"It was another dead end." Literally. The plate was registered to a dead man.

Sande closed her eyes, fighting the need to burst into tears, if the trembling of her lips was any indication. She sat next to him in Cates's office. The detective had stepped out to confer with his captain.

Patrick shouldn't, but he couldn't help himself. He reached out, put his hand on her clasped ones. "We'll figure this out."

Her eyes flew open. There was nothing soft or vulnerable about the emotion glittering there. She'd had enough.

"How will we do that?" She blinked, visibly struggling to regain her composure. "Everyone involved with this case ends up dead."

Before Patrick could console her with some mundane assurance about how he would make certain nothing happened to her, Cates returned. The detective planted himself in the chair behind his desk and spread what appeared to be a number of reports in front of him.

"My captain has authorized me to share some of the details of this case with you."

Patrick didn't mention that Lyons had already done that. There was always the chance that he hadn't given as many details as Cates would. Or in some way misrepresented the information. Having it relayed from a second source couldn't hurt.

"I appreciate your cooperation, Detective."

"There's not a lot to tell." Cates scanned the reports in front of him. "My partner's file was fairly incomplete."

That surprised Patrick. He'd seen the file Lyons had amassed. Incomplete was far from what he would have called it. "Really?"

Cates gestured to the papers before him. "This is all there is."

Next to Patrick, Sande tensed. The shift in posture was subtle, but he noticed. She'd seen the size of the file when Lyons had brought it into the interview room.

"I'm sure whatever you have will be helpful," Patrick stated.

Cates reviewed the number of victims from the three metro areas involved. He mentioned the Bureau's involvement again.

"Your partner didn't say anything about the FBI," Patrick pointed out once more, hoping the detective might clear up that issue.

Cates made a face, one that reflected his frustration. "I'm looking at a report from his Bureau counterpart." He passed it to Patrick. "I don't know why he wouldn't have mentioned that." He shrugged. "Unless the Bureau didn't want their involvement discussed with outside sources. There's always that chance."

Special Agent Chet Wheeler. The agent's cell phone number was listed in the report. Patrick committed it to memory. His next call would be to Agent Wheeler. He passed the report back to Cates. "Has Wheeler been contacted regarding your partner's murder?"

"I've left three voice mails," Cates said with another heavy dose of frustration. "The man has yet to return my call."

That wasn't like the Bureau. The Colby Agency worked with the Chicago field office on a regular basis and never experienced a glitch.

Cates leaned back in his chair and fixed Patrick

with a look that said things were about to get complicated. "Your client—" he glanced at Sande "—is the only lead we've got in this mess. My captain thinks it would be in her best interest to go into protective custody until we figure this out."

"You realize the Colby Agency has her best interests covered," Patrick reminded him.

"You realize," Cates countered, "that Chicago PD is far better prepared to handle the job."

Sande looked from Patrick to Cates and back. "Do I have a say in the matter?"

When Cates would have answered, Patrick cut him off. "Of course you do." To the detective's surprise, he added, "Detective Cates does have a point, however. Tucking you away in a safe house would lessen the risk to you."

Sande shook her head adamantly. "I'll stick with the Colby Agency."

"Ms. Williams," Cates argued, "are you sure about that? We've had three homicides in the past twenty-four hours. All somehow related to this case—" he tapped one of the reports "—and you."

Confusion and uncertainty were visible on Sande's face. "But how can I find out what happened to me if I'm locked away somewhere?"

"We could hold you," Cates pressed, but Patrick took the floor.

"Other than her name, you actually can't connect Ms. Williams to any of these murders."

"You mean," Cates rebutted, "other than the fact that each of the victims was contacted in some manner by one or both of you only hours before they were murdered?"

"Come on, Detective, you know as well as I do that's nothing more than coincidence."

"One victim is coincidence, Mr. O'Brien," Cates retorted. "Three…" He shook his head. "No way."

Patrick stood. "Levy charges or back off." He turned to Sande. "Let's go."

"I want to go on record, O'Brien," Cates called, before he could hustle Sande out the door.

Patrick turned back to the man.

"I think you're making a mistake." The detective tilted his head so that he could look past Patrick to where Sande stood. "I might not have any evidence, lady, but my gut says you're living on borrowed time. I think I'd hedge my bets by going into protective custody."

"Good day, Detective." Patrick turned his back and escorted Sande out of the building.

As soon as they were in the car headed away from the precinct, Sande spoke up. "What do we do now?"

"Remember that receptionist at Peyton and Wyatt?"

"Definitely." Hope rose in her voice once more.

"Do you think we could talk to her outside the office? She might open up if she doesn't have to fear any repercussions from her boss."

"Exactly." Patrick sent Sande a warm smile. For a civilian she was damned good at this. "I'll ask Windy to track her down and see how receptive she is to talking." He took a right at the next intersection. "Meanwhile, we're going to visit Agent Wheeler and find out why he's not returning the voice mails Cates left."

And anything else Patrick could prompt from the seemingly behind-the-scenes agent.

Patrick entered the number he had memorized into his cell, expecting to get Wheeler's answering machine. To his surprise, the agent answered.

Even more surprising, he was quite willing to meet with them. Now. All they had to do was name the place.

Special Agent Wheeler's training obviously hadn't included one primary element the Colby Agency's training covered thoroughly: always assume the home field advantage.

The Colby Agency.

Patrick's home turf.

HER HEART THUMPING WILDLY, Sande stepped off the elevator into the Colby Agency lobby.

*Wow.* She had expected nice, but this went way beyond nice. Lush carpeting and deep, rich colors.

Classic fine furnishings. The atmosphere evoked a sense of welcome, as well as an assurance that only the very best would call this place home.

"Patrick, Agent Wheeler is waiting in your office," the receptionist announced as O'Brien passed her desk.

He thanked her without pausing. Sande scarcely had time to return the woman's smile as she hurried to keep up with O'Brien's long strides.

At the door to his office he stopped and waited for her to enter first. Sande walked, part of her hoping to glean something about the man from his work environment. But instead, her attention was snagged by the visitor standing on the other side of the room, staring out the window. There was something vaguely familiar about his posture and the color of his hair…

He turned around slowly.

Sande's breath caught.

*It was him.*

The man she'd seen in the coffee shop.

The one she was certain she knew from somewhere.

Special Agent Wheeler smiled broadly and reached up to remove his dark eyewear. "Mr. O'Brien." He settled his gaze on Sande. "Ms. Williams. I had hoped we could come together like this."

Somehow, Sande managed to sit down in the closest chair. She wasn't sure how much longer her legs would have held her upright.

How did she know this man?

Equal parts fire and ice rushed over her skin. She couldn't decide if she was freezing or burning up. A sharp pain pierced deep inside her skull.

O'Brien offered his hand to their visitor. "I'm certain we've met, Agent Wheeler," he said, his tone all business and nothing short of direct. "You look vaguely familiar to me."

Sande didn't know if O'Brien recognized him from the coffee shop or if he was merely fishing.

"We have, indeed, Mr. O'Brien." Wheeler shook the offered hand, then shifted his eyes toward Sande. "At the coffee shop this morning. I noticed the two of you there when I made my morning stop."

"Have you spoken to Detective Cates in the last hour?" O'Brien gestured for him to have a seat as he rounded his desk.

"Yes." The agent lowered himself into a chair near Sande. "I spoke with him perhaps ten minutes ago."

"Then you know Detective Lyons was murdered this morning."

Wheeler gave a nod of acknowledgment. "Tragic."

Sande watched the man, finding his cool demeanor infuriated her beyond reason.

O'Brien nodded. "Yes, tragic is an apt description."

Wheeler crossed one leg over the over and leaned back in his seat as if he owned the meeting. "Cates mentioned that you had questions regarding the case Detective Lyons and I were working."

The rest of the conversation was lost on Sande. She couldn't stop staring at the man. She *knew* him. Somehow. His mannerisms. His bearing. Everything about him was innately familiar.

Her thoughts jolted back to the conversation just as Agent Wheeler stood, announcing the meeting was over.

"Feel free to call if there's any way I can assist your investigation, Mr. O'Brien." He turned to Sande. "Ms. Williams, good luck with your quest." He slipped his sunglasses back into place and walked away.

Confused, Sande looked at O'Brien. "I was a little preoccupied just now. But did we learn anything? I mean—" she glanced toward the door the agent had only moments ago vanished through "—he was in and out with scarcely a sentence between."

O'Brien appeared almost as confused as Sande felt. "We now know that the Bureau was allowing Lyons to lead on this one. Wheeler claims his only interest in the case was in an advisory capacity. That's it."

The pain that had started deep in her skull started to throb in time with the pounding in her chest. "Do you believe him?" Wheeler had shown up at the coffee shop that morning as if he had known they would be there. Then he'd driven away in a car registered to a dead man. This was wrong. So, so, so wrong.

"Come on." O'Brien skirted his desk.

"Where're we going?" Her head was still spinning from the agent's bizarre hit-and-run.

"We're going straight to the horse's mouth."

Sande followed O'Brien back toward the lobby. "Meaning?"

"The Bureau." O'Brien pushed the elevator call button. "I want to speak to Wheeler's superior. I want confirmation from the top."

Sande decided they should hurry. Otherwise Wheeler could end up dead, too.

Cates should watch his back as well, she mused. Every damned body they had talked to so far ended up that way.

As FRUSTRATING AS getting past security at Peyton and Wyatt had been, it turned out to be a piece of cake compared to getting past the Bureau's security.

Sande Williams didn't exist as far as the FBI was concerned. The DMV information utilized to obtain her driver's license was of little consequence in their eyes. After fingerprinting and a background check, all of which took approximately fifty minutes, she was finally admitted onto the Bureau's sacred ground.

Special Agent in Charge Dennis Young was more

than happy to take time out of his busy day to see an investigator from the Colby Agency. But that was where the good news began and ended.

Young shook his head. "Mr. O'Brien, I'm afraid you've stumped me. We have no one here that matches the description you and Ms. Williams gave of the man with whom you spoke."

O'Brien studied Young for several beats. "You're saying you don't have an Agent Wheeler at this field office?"

"That's correct."

"What about at another field office?"

Young gave another of those adamant head shakes. "Let me clarify this for you once and for all." He buzzed his secretary and asked for the personnel file on Wheeler.

"But you said you don't have an Agent Wheeler," O'Brien stated.

Young held up a hand signaling him to hold on.

Sande waited, her heartbeat stumbling. Like everything else in her life since she'd woken up on that gurney, this did not add up.

When the secretary provided Young with the file he'd requested, he opened the folder and pushed it across the desk for O'Brien's perusal.

"That," Young said, reaching across his desk to tap an eight-by-ten photo, "is Special Agent Chet Wheeler."

The Chet Wheeler in the photograph was older than the man who had come to O'Brien's office. Sande leaned forward to get a closer look. Definitely not the same person.

"I don't understand." O'Brien looked from the file to the agent in charge. "First you tell me you don't have an Agent Wheeler, then you show me his file. If this agent is on staff here, I'd like to speak with him."

Sande imagined O'Brien was thinking the same thing she was. The guy who had shown up at his office could have been masquerading as Wheeler for reasons she couldn't begin to fathom. Then again, Young insisted Wheeler didn't exist. It was too crazy for her.

Young closed the file and dragged it back to his side of the desk. "I'm afraid that's impossible, Mr. O'Brien."

Patrick O'Brien generally kept his face clear of emotion, but not this time. Frustration was etched on every plane and angle.

"I think it's a reasonable request, considering what's at stake for my client."

"Chet Wheeler is dead, Mr. O'Brien," Young said flatly. "He was killed in the line of duty. *Two years ago.*"

The rest of the exchange was lost on Sande.

She felt numb as she and O'Brien left the building.

Dead. Dead. Dead.

Everyone was dead.

As she climbed into the car, O'Brien took a call

on his cell phone. Sande leaned back in her seat and closed her eyes. She felt exhausted. She couldn't take any more. When would this nightmare be over?

And when it was, who would be left?

"We may have gotten a break."

Sande opened her eyes and sat up straighter. "What?"

O'Brien shot her a faint smile. "That was Windy. The receptionist from Peyton and Wyatt has agreed to talk to us. Windy's waiting for us at her apartment."

Finally. A step in the right direction.

# *Chapter Eleven*

*Lincoln Park*

Kitty Grant lived in an apartment building in the Lincoln Park neighborhood. According to Windy, she had lived there since starting at Peyton and Wyatt four years ago. She had no children and was unmarried. Peyton and Wyatt was her first job out of college.

The receptionist had admitted to recognizing Sande, but refused to say more until she and Sande were face-to-face. Patrick could understand her hesitation. She was afraid for her job, probably for her life, considering the number of people who had been murdered in the past thirty or so hours.

The bodies just kept piling up.

And he and his client were getting nowhere.

Windy's car was parked in the visitor's space next to the one designated for apartment 331. Patrick parked two slots away and led Sande into the building, to the third floor. The complex had no security as far as he could see. But the neighborhood was a good one, so there was no compelling reason for a prospective tenant to seek out a more secure property.

At the door marked 331, he knocked. The silence in the corridor, as well as on the other side of the wooden panel sent his instincts on alert.

"If I was ever employed by Peyton and Wyatt," Sande said quietly, "the receptionist would've had to see me on a regular basis."

"Unquestionably." Patrick hoped that would be the case. So far, however, this investigation had gone any way but as expected.

He hoped for Sande's sake that pattern was about to change.

When there was no answer after a second knock, Patrick put through a call to Windy's cell phone. No answer there, either.

A distant muffled sound caused him to frown. He entered Windy's number a second time and waited, then heard the sound again.

Cell phone.

Windy's.

Patrick grasped the knob and twisted.

The door opened without resistance.

He pushed it wide and listened.

The muffled rings were louder now. One more and the call went to voice mail.

With an alarm going off in his head, Patrick stepped cautiously through the doorway. "Stay behind me," he ordered Sande.

Three steps farther and he understood why no one had answered the door or his call.

He shoved his phone at Sande. "Call 9-1-1."

Patrick dropped to a crouch next to Windy, who lay facedown on the floor. He closed his eyes and fought the emotion that accompanied the confirmation that she was dead.

Kitty Grant was dead as well.

Each woman had taken one shot to the back of the head.

Patrick stood. He turned all the way around, emotions funneling inside him.

He should check the apartment.

Make sure it was clear. Make sure it was safe for Sande to be here.

Ensure there was nothing useful to his case lying in plain sight.

But he could do none of that.

Windy Millwood was dead.

Agony erupted deep in his chest.

To his knowledge the Colby Agency had never lost an investigator.

Until today.

# Chapter Twelve

Victoria Colby-Camp had taken the helm of the Colby Agency after her husband's murder. More than twenty years had passed since then. Her personal life had fallen apart twice over and been rebuilt. The original home of the agency had been destroyed and rebuilt. Investigators had suffered heartache and physical injury. They had come and gone, always keeping in touch from wherever life took them.

But not once in all those years had one been lost.

Windy Millwood's death would not be for naught.

Victoria would see that her killer was found and brought to justice. She would also see to it that Sande Williams got her life back. However long it took, whatever the cost.

Victoria considered the investigator seated on the other side of her desk. She knew the pain he was feeling all too well. Regret, guilt. He had sent Windy in search of the receptionist. He had walked into a murder scene with a client in tow, without ensuring that it was safe to do so.

He had made mistakes.

"Patrick," she said, her voice surprisingly strong despite the emotion tearing at her insides, "your only misstep was in allowing the client to follow you into an uncertain situation. You have carried out the responsibilities of your assignment to the best of your ability. As did Windy. You did not ask her to do anything she would not have asked you to do had circumstances been reversed."

He swallowed with effort. His throat would be dry. His head likely ached. His gut was probably in knots. And his chest would feel as if it might explode.

She knew all the symptoms.

"The only question now," Victoria continued, "is are you able to complete your assignment?" She drew in a bolstering breath. "If you feel you are not, that's perfectly understandable, as you well know. Ian or Simon will step in for you without question or hesitation. Lucas has taken a personal interest in this case and is working with a contact he believes might be able to shed some light on the involvement of our federal friends. The Bureau may not be the agency involved."

Patrick found his voice. "With all due respect, Victoria, I would prefer to remain on the case." His gaze connected fully with hers. "Unless you've lost confidence in my ability to finish the job."

She shook her head. "Not at all, Patrick. It would be my preference for you to complete your assignment. The client has developed trust in you, and in this case, that's particularly important."

He stood. "Very well. I'd like to get back to my investigation now."

"Simon will provide any backup you need," Victoria explained. "Under the circumstances I'd like you to report in as often as possible."

Patrick nodded and turned toward the door, but hesitated before opening it and walking out. A moment passed before he spoke. "Thank you."

The words were scarcely more than a whisper.

"For?" Victoria could feel the tension radiating from him all the way across her office. Her own emotions were barely held in check.

His dark eyes collided with hers again. "For allowing me the opportunity to get this bastard first."

Patrick O'Brien walked out of Victoria's office.

Despite his years of formal training in recognizing and understanding the behaviors of the human psyche, he was as human as she or anyone else.

He wanted revenge.

He wanted justice.

Victoria had taken care of notifying Windy's

family and the man she'd dated for nearly two years. The funeral would be in three days. Anything Windy's family needed would be taken care of by the Colby Agency. Everyone on staff would be in attendance at the funeral.

And for the first time in nearly twenty-five years, the Colby Agency would be closed on a workday.

Victoria cradled her face in her hands and did something she hadn't done in a very long time.

She cried.

For the waste of such a lovely, intelligent young woman's life.

For the anguish that would stay with Patrick O'Brien for the rest of his.

# *Chapter Thirteen*

Patrick took Victoria's advice and sought refuge for Sande and himself at the Colby Agency safe house. The spacious, exquisite house perched on the lake-shore had once been home to Victoria and her first husband, James Colby. But after their only child, Jim, had gone missing and James had been murdered, Victoria had refused to return to the place she'd called home. The house had sat empty for years until it was put into use as a safe house, to shelter a client.

Like now.

"Explore the place if you want to," Patrick told Sande as she turned around in the well-appointed entry hall. "Pick any room you'd like on the second floor."

He placed their bags at the bottom of the staircase. He needed coffee. And then he needed to think about how to proceed from here.

He armed the security system and headed for the

kitchen. When he'd set the coffeemaker to brew, he braced his arms against the counter and stared out the window above the sink. Moonlight glistened on the dark waters of the lake.

He'd been here once or twice.

With Windy.

She'd been his mentor for the past year. Showing him the ropes of how things were done at the Colby Agency. He'd met her boyfriend a couple of times. Nice guy. Totally the opposite of Windy. He taught school, coached Little League in the summer. He'd wanted to get married months ago, but Windy kept putting him off. She wasn't ready to make that leap.

Now she would never have the chance.

"This is a beautiful place."

Sande's voice startled Patrick from the painful thoughts. He straightened, forced his mind back to the present and his job. "Very beautiful." And filled with tormenting memories for Victoria. Even now she never came. All this beauty and she couldn't bear to be here.

"You made coffee."

Patrick shook off the haunting thoughts. "Yes." Sande didn't drink coffee. "Sorry. Would you like tea?" He had to get his mind wrapped around the case again.

"I'm fine for now." She hugged her arms around

herself as she stared out over the water. "Mostly I'm tired. And sad for being the reason Windy's dead."

He shook his head. "Don't. That won't help."

The shaky breath she released told him that nothing he said would relieve her of the guilt she felt for this. Just like him.

He shouldn't put off this other thing any longer. "I wanted to discuss a technique with you." He poured a cup of coffee. "If you're not too tired."

Hope chased away the weariness in her expression. "Will it help me remember?"

"Possibly." He walked to the table and took a seat. She did the same. "I can't guarantee anything, but at this point, I believe it's worth a try."

He'd been thinking about this for a while now. Many therapists swore by hypnotherapy, but Patrick wasn't one of them. So many unscrupulous practitioners in his field used it as a cure-all, knowing full well it rarely worked to any real degree.

But it couldn't hurt.

"Tell me," she urged.

"It's called regression therapy." He avoided the more common term.

A frown furrowed her smooth brow. "I'm not sure what that involves."

"It's fairly simple and straightforward." He savored his coffee. "I use hypnosis to take you back to a time you remember, then we slowly move forward until we reach the present."

She pondered his suggestion for nearly a minute before she responded. Patrick had assumed she would be willing to try most anything. Maybe he'd been wrong.

"Okay." She looked directly into his eyes. "When can we start?"

Relief warred with prudence. He wanted to be glad she'd agreed, but a part of him would prefer not to take this route. He thought of Windy and his hesitation vanished. He would do whatever necessary to nail his associate and friend's killer.

In answer to Sande's question, he said, "I'd like you to treat yourself to a long, hot bath, get as relaxed as possible and then we'll start."

"There's no time like the present." She stood and backed toward the hall. "It's not like it's going to be a hardship. A long, hot bath sounds really good." She disappeared in the direction of the stairs.

Patrick hoped she would feel that way later. Regression therapy could be emotionally agonizing for those patients for whom it really worked. There were some who didn't respond to hypnosis. An unguarded response was key to achieving the best results.

The Colby Agency research department had found nothing on Sande Williams. The police had nothing.

Evidently the Bureau had nothing. Anyone who might have known something had ended up dead.

Patrick was out of options. If this didn't work, he wasn't sure there was anything else he could do to help the lady. And then finding the person responsible for Windy's murder might just be impossible.

SANDE SELECTED the bedroom with the largest tub. There was even a big, fluffy white robe on the back of the door. She filled the bath with steaming water and sprinkled in some of the essence of rose oil she'd found in the linen closest.

She dropped the robe onto the floor next to a couple of matching towels, and twisted and clipped her hair out of the way. Taking her time, she gingerly stepped into the water. The sensation of warmth swallowing her body felt amazing. Her bottom settled against the porcelain and she leaned back with a satisfied sigh.

Slowly but surely she banished the ugly images of murder from her mind. Those awful pictures of Windy lying facedown on the floor, of O'Brien trying desperately to help her, were the hardest to exile. That this woman had died because of her made Sande sick to her stomach. Who else had to perish before this was over?

Maybe if she herself had died the way she was

supposed to have, Windy and Alma and Nancy, not to mention Detective Lyons, would still be alive.

Emotion welled in Sande's eyes. What had happened in her life to create this domino effect? Who was she? What kind of people did she associate with? Obviously, the sort who could kill without blinking an eye.

Why would she have associates like that? What kind of evil person had she been?

Sande told herself to relax, but it didn't work. She needed answers. Why couldn't she remember? The lab hadn't been able to pinpoint any drugs in her system. She had no physical injuries. If her memory had fled due to some emotional trauma, then that should stop.

She had to be stronger. There was no excuse for her continued hiding. And that's what this was, wasn't it?

She was a coward.

"Not anymore." Sande pushed herself out of the hot water and grabbed a towel. She scrubbed her body dry and then dragged on the robe. Enough time had been wasted.

She didn't need to relax. She needed to get this done.

Determined, Sande stormed off in search of O'Brien. She was ready to get this over with. Whatever he could dig from her brain, using whatever methods, she wanted to try it.

Now.

She found him in the kitchen where she'd left him, cup of coffee still in his hand. Judging by the fullness of the carafe, he hadn't gotten to his second cup.

"I'm ready."

His attention snapped to her. Surprised flared in his eyes. "That was pretty fast. The goal was to relax."

She pulled out the chair she had abandoned earlier. "I'm as relaxed as I'm going to get. Let's get started."

Now she was mad at him, too. Her feelings were irrational, she knew. But she just couldn't help it. Her *life* was irrational right now.

"All right." O'Brien got up from the table. "Let's find a spot more conducive to relaxing."

"Whatever."

Sande followed him to the living room. He started the gas logs in the fireplace. Then he settled into a massive wingback chair that flanked one side, gesturing to the matching seat opposite. Sande dropped into it and pulled her legs up so that she could hug her knees to her chest. She liked sitting that way. With the fluffy robe cloaking her, she had to admit she felt warm and somewhat relaxed in spite of her anger.

Patrick blinked away the appealing image of

her sitting there swallowed in that white robe, with her blond hair spilling loose from its confines. He had to focus.

Slowly, methodically, he talked her to that place where her mind drifted deep, deep into the past.

Her gaze softened, grew distant.

"Very good, Sande."

She sighed, sank deeper into the fluffy folds of white swaddling her.

"Tell me about your birthday, Sande."

She tugged on her bottom lip with those straight white teeth. Patrick's body tensed. He pushed away the sensations.

"I…was ten," she murmured.

"Ten. That's a pleasant age."

"It's snowing."

So, she was born in the winter. "Where was it snowing, Sande?" He kept his voice low, gentle.

"Minneapolis."

Excellent.

"You grew up in Minneapolis."

"Yes."

Her skin was almost as pale as the robe. Smooth. Her lips looked as rich as plums against her skin. And young, she looked so young.

*Focus,* he ordered himself.

"Did the kids in school laugh at your glasses?"

A frown tugged at those full lips. "I didn't wear glasses." She inclined her head. "They laughed at my braces."

"When did you get braces, Sande?"

"I was fourteen."

"Fourteen. A time of change." He chose his words carefully, steering away from those that might generate unpleasant memories, yet selecting ones that would prompt reaction.

"I bought my first bra."

He smiled despite his determination to maintain a professional facade. "There are many firsts when you're a teenager."

"I let Josh Baker kiss me after the pep rally."

Another smile pulled at his lips. "You were a cheerleader?"

She moved her head from side to side. "No. I was in the band. I played the flute."

"The flute is a nice instrument."

"I hated it. My mother made me play."

"Did she make you get a job after you graduated?"

The soft expression transitioned into a pained look. "No. She died."

An ache pierced Patrick's chest. "I'm very sorry, Sande."

Her expression changed again. "Why do you keep calling me Sande?"

Tension rippled through his limbs. "Isn't that your name? Sande Williams?"

Confusion or something of that order pinched her face. "No. That's not my name."

*Take a detour.* "Isn't that the name you used in college?"

She shook her head. "Of course not. Why would I use that name? It's not mine."

"Maybe you've forgotten," he suggested with a bit more firmness.

"No. I didn't forget. Angela Tapley. That's my name."

Anticipation prompted an adrenaline surge. "I see. Well, Angela, what did you do after college?"

A full minute passed and she said nothing. The remote expression that had claimed her face and eyes told him she was looking back…searching of her own volition through the memories imprinted on her cells.

A new kind of tension mounted when the silent seconds continued to tick by.

"I was ranked first in my class," she finally announced. "No one was better. Not even Ted Baxley. He thought he was the best, but he wasn't. I was."

"You were valedictorian?"

"Not college. My training cycle."

Patrick sat forward. "I see. You joined the military."

"No." Frustration had seeped into her tone. "At the Farm."

Comprehension set off a whole new blast of adrenaline. "You joined the Bureau after college."

"Special Agent Angela Tapley."

Patrick was the one silent now. Her answer had stunned him.

*Don't get distracted. Finish this.*

"Your last operation went south," he commented, careful to keep his inflection neutral.

His client shot to her feet. "He's dead. I killed him."

Patrick searched her face, her eyes, wondered at the confusion and anguish there. She was still in the past. "You killed who?"

"Wheeler," she murmured. "But he just won't stay dead."

Patrick slowly pushed himself to his feet and approached her. *No sudden moves.* "Why did you need to kill him?"

"Because he's responsible."

The tension in her posture told him she was ready to cut and run. Not good. "How was he responsible?"

"He's a traitor."

She was shaking now.

"I'm going to count very slowly from ten to one," Patrick told her. "When I get to one you're going to feel relaxed again. Then you'll wake up and have tea."

She gazed at him as if she didn't understand.

"Ten…nine…eight…"

The shaking didn't abate.

"Are you listening to me, Sande?"

"Don't call me that!" She backed up a step.

"Seven…almost time to relax and wake up."

She stared at him, her eyes unseeing.

"Six…five…four…you'll remember what we talked about, but you won't be afraid."

She stumbled back a step, crumpled into the chair she'd abandoned minutes ago.

"Three…two…*one*." Patrick crouched next to her. "You okay?"

She turned to look directly into his eyes. "I'm not sure." Her voice sound calm if not steady. Her gaze was still somewhat distant.

"Do you remember your name?"

More of those tension-filled seconds stretched out.

"My name is Angela Tapley."

The shaking started again.

"You're tired. Why don't you let me take you to your bedroom?"

She didn't resist. Patrick helped her up the stairs and into the room where she'd discarded her clothes. He drew the covers back and waited for her to crawl into the bed. As he tucked her in, his mind was already racing with what he needed to do next.

"O'Brien."

He hesitated at her bedside. "Yes?"

"How can I remember my name and not know what happened to me?"

He'd hoped, after she rested, to learn more about what she'd done since joining the Bureau, but that apparently wasn't going to happen right away.

"It'll come. Try to rest now. You're tired. I'll take care of everything."

Even as he made the promise his gut twisted into writhing knots of agony.

The way he'd taken care of his wife.

The way he'd taken care of Windy.

Maybe Victoria had been on the right track when she'd suggested that Ian or Simon should take over this case.

Frustration and anger joined the self-disgust.

When his client had drifted off to sleep, he left the room. He had calls to make. A plan to develop.

His cell phone was vibrating on the kitchen table. He grabbed it on the way to the coffeemaker. More caffeine was essential.

"O'Brien."

"O'Brien, this is Simon."

Simon Ruhl. He and Ian Michaels were Victoria's seconds in command. Patrick's instincts went on point. "I have news," he informed his superior. "Our client's real name is Angela Tapley."

"She's FBI," Simon added. Simon was former FBI himself.

"I just learned that through regression therapy," Patrick explained. "What's your source?"

"Lucas's contact uncovered a black bag operation. All hell is about to break loose at the Bureau. You'll need to be on your toes, O'Brien. This is going to get nasty."

"I'm prepared." He'd packed his weapon. Patrick had never carried a gun before, but he'd been trained by the Colby Agency and issued a 9 mm for extreme situations. Few of the investigators at the agency ever carried their weapon, much less used it.

"Ian is on his way there now. Once your backup is in place I'll give you another call and fill you in on the rest of what we learned. Right now we all need to focus on getting this situation locked down for the coming ride."

"I'll be standing by."

Patrick put the phone away and ran his hand through his hair. He had to push all the remorse and guilt about Windy out of his mind until this was done. He would deal with it then. For now, his top priority had to be protecting the client.

His throat went dry when he thought of those lush

lips and the glimpses of thigh he'd gotten whenever she moved or walked in that robe. He'd had to work hard at not letting his attention deviate from the task.

He reminded himself that he was confusing the need to protect with other emotions. It happened. He knew better than to succumb.

But he was merely human.

He downed his coffee, refilled his cup and decided to check the house and security system, even though he knew the latter was state-of-the-art and that all was well. It would keep him occupied until Ian arrived.

Otherwise he'd be focusing on those thoughts that would only take him places he did not need to go.

"Don't move."

Patrick froze.

"Put your hands up and turn around slowly."

*What the hell?*

"I said, put your hands up and turn around slowly."

He raised his hands in classic surrender and swiveled slowly.

His gaze settled on Sande's—Angela's—face. Her eyes were wild with fear or something of that order. She was still wearing that fluffy white robe, but the gun in her hand took away any fragile look. "What're you doing with the weapon?" he asked quietly. "You're supposed to be resting."

She tightened her grip on the 9 mm she'd obviously taken from his bag. Her hands shook. "Shut up! And don't make any sudden moves."

"Sande."

"Don't call me that!" Her lips trembled despite the hard line she'd pressed them into. "Don't ever call me that again."

"Listen to me," he urged gently. "I'm trying to help you. You know you can trust me."

She laughed. "Yeah, right. The last guy I trusted tried to have me killed." She lifted her chin in defiance of those trembling lips. "I don't think I'll be making that mistake again."

"You have to let me help you." Patrick hesitated to call her Angela. He wasn't sure what kind of emotion that would evoke.

"I have to think," she practically shouted. "I…" She moistened her lips and dragged in a ragged breath. "I have to think."

"Put the weapon away and we'll work this out."

She stared straight down the barrel at him. "Not a chance. You do exactly what I tell you or you're dead. Got it?"

Patrick nodded. "Got it."

If Ian picked now to arrive…someone would likely end up dead.

## *Chapter Fourteen*

Sande…*Angela*.

Her name was Angela.

She had to remember that.

The operation had gone south.

Where the hell was she?

She stared at the man in front of her. Peyton…no, Patrick. Patrick O'Brien. She'd been with him for a few days now.

Nancy was dead.

Alma, too.

She shuddered. Felt cold. Sick. She needed to throw up. Why was everyone dead? Something had gone wrong.

Had to be him.

She leveled her aim on the man in front of her. This had to be his fault.

Flashes of memory slammed into her brain. *Him*

keeping her close behind him. *Him* putting his hand on hers. *Him* trying to help Alma…and the others.

She closed her eyes, fought the confusion.

What was he doing with her?

"Everyone at the Colby Agency wants to help you."

She opened her eyes. Stared at the man who had spoken. *Colby Agency.* The old woman who lived in the boxes, from that day she had escaped. She'd been naked. She'd awakened by the morgue.

And then he had come to help her.

Patrick O'Brien. The man whose wife had cheated on him, then gotten herself murdered. The man who promised to keep her safe.

The man who had kept his promise.

Angela dropped to her knees. The gun clattered to the floor.

And then she cried.

Cried for the people who had lost their lives because of her. She still didn't know why, but she knew with complete certainty that it was all her fault.

"You're safe."

His whispered voice touched her in a place that had been empty and cold for so long she could scarcely draw in her next breath.

No one had been there when she needed help.

No one had come to save her.

She'd been left alone. Abandoned when the operation had fallen apart.

Patrick O'Brien pulled her into his arms and cradled her like a child. She burrowed into the warmth and security he offered.

No one had held her this way in so very long.

She needed someone to help her. This man had promised to do that. She had to trust him.

She couldn't do this alone anymore.

Patrick gathered the sobbing woman into his arms and carried her upstairs. He placed her on the bed in the room she'd chosen, and pulled the covers up around her.

The cell phone in his pocket vibrated. "I'll be right back," he promised before leaving her.

In the hall outside her room he took the call. "O'Brien."

"Any problems inside?"

Ian Michaels.

Patrick let go a big breath. "No." He swallowed at the tightness in his throat. "No problems. I've got everything under control in here."

"I've taken up a post on the opposite side of the street. Shane Allen will be here momentarily to assume a post behind the house."

"Thanks, Ian."

Patrick closed the phone and sagged against the wall. He scrubbed a hand over his face and tried to clear the fog from his brain. Three years ago he had sworn he would never let himself be deceived again. Although Sande Williams—Angela Tapley—had not purposely deceived him, he'd fallen under her spell to some degree and that was not good.

He'd gotten too close, too personally involved, and his years of formal education had gone right out the window, just like last time.

He was on his way back to the kitchen when his cell vibrated again. It would be Simon with word on what he'd learned from Lucas's contact. Patrick pulled himself together and took the call. "O'Brien."

"O'Brien, if you're in a position for me to bring you up to speed, we'll get that done."

Patrick returned to the bottom of the stairs and listened a moment. All quiet. Hopefully Angela—he still had trouble calling her that—was sleeping. "Now's good. Go ahead."

"According to Lucas's contact, a shadow operation, what the CIA would refer to as a black bag operation, was set in motion three years ago."

Patrick had some idea of what all that meant, but wanted the full story. "What exactly does that entail?"

"That means it's off the record. Conducted in the dark. No support or contact with the Bureau whatsoever. No one knows except the director himself and the field agent in charge of the operation. The

Bureau rarely does an operation like this. They leave that kind of cloak-and-dagger stuff to the CIA."

Sounded risky for the agents involved.

"This particular operation was put in place to infiltrate an organization here in Chicago that specialized in stealing identities. But those in charge of the thriving organization decided to branch out and delve into other illegal activities."

"Such as?"

"Data miners."

That sounded like something his computer's firewall blocked. "How do these data miners work?"

"The desired identity is located. For example, if the job required a certain educational background or work history, the identity is chosen and taken. One of the organization's many soldiers assumes the identity and accepts a position at, say, Peyton and Wyatt."

Now the picture came into focus. "That soldier," Patrick guessed, "uses his or her position to gather information for the stealing."

"Then that person would simply disappear or return to his or her normal life. We believe Nancy Childers was one of those soldiers. We don't know why some were executed. Perhaps all were. The firm…"

"Angela was working undercover to help infiltrate this organization?" Patrick didn't actually need confirmation; the rest was easy to guess. If Nancy Childers had in fact been one of them, she'd been damned good at concealing her reactions.

"Yes. Angela was one of two agents from the D.C. office assigned to work here under Chet Wheeler, just over two years ago. Angela was selected because of her specialized training in software systems. One month ago she disappeared, and no one has seen or heard from her until now. Because she was involved in a shadow operation, her personnel file for all intents and purposes didn't exist. That's why her prints didn't garner a match. But as soon as we ran them, the director's office was notified."

"Why didn't the Bureau step forward and retrieve their agent?" Patrick didn't like the idea that she had been left to sink or swim even after the FBI learned that she was still alive and right here in Chicago.

"That's the sticky part," Simon explained. "They need this operation to play out. The ultimate goal is far too important to jeopardize for one agent."

They were going to use her as bait. "Can Lucas talk to someone and let them know that their agent is in no condition to finish what she started? Right now she's more than a little unstable. This needs to end. Now."

"He's already tried that. Didn't work. This is the

way they do things, O'Brien. Your job is to react to whatever is thrown your way. And to keep her safe to the best of your ability."

"I don't like it." Patrick recognized when he was bested. There was nothing he could do but, as Simon said, react.

"I'll check in with you every hour," his colleague informed him before ending the call.

Patrick gave his word that he wouldn't go changing the game plan. But he wasn't sure he could stick by his promise.

He'd always done the right thing, and it hadn't always worked. Maybe he would follow his gut this time instead of the rules.

That was exactly what Windy would do. She would follow her instincts. Patrick owed it to her to do the job the way she would.

And get the bad guys.

SHE WAS RUNNING.

The sheet flapped against her bare thighs.

She had to run faster. He would catch her otherwise. And then she would be finished.

Fingers closed around her throat. She gasped for breath. He was winning!

She couldn't escape this time…

Angela bolted upright in bed, her breath rasping in and out of her lungs, and looked around the room.

*Safe.* She was safe.

Safe house.

The Colby Agency was protecting her.

Her heart rate slowed little by little.

*Okay.* She was okay.

He couldn't get her here.

She shoved the hair back from her face and slowed her breathing. *Deep breath, release. Another. Long, deep breath. Let it go. Calm. Find that calm place.*

Throwing the covers back, she dropped her bare feet to the floor. She stood on shaky legs and righted the robe twisted around her torso.

O'Brien.

God, she'd pulled a gun on him.

He probably wasn't very happy with her right now. She had some explaining to do.

She should get dressed.

Angela fished some underwear and jeans from the bag Windy had prepared for her.

*Windy.*

Anguish pierced her. Windy was dead because of her. Alma, Nancy, they were all dead. But then Nancy had been one of them. Alma, however, had been an innocent victim, guilty of nothing but being a nosy neighbor.

*Suck it up. Don't think about it.*

She couldn't finish this if she allowed herself to sink into the pain.

And she couldn't let *him* win.

After tugging a sweater over her head, she dug around for socks, then found her shoes.

Who *he* was still remained unclear, but she would lure him out into the open and take him down.

She had survived what he'd done to her. That fact alone was an outright miracle. There had to be a reason God had ensured that she live.

She found O'Brien downstairs, talking on the phone. He flipped it shut and turned to meet her as she approached.

For several moments she couldn't bring herself to speak. He'd risked his life and that of his associate to protect her. To help her uncover her past. Only to learn that she was not who or what he'd thought.

A man who had been deceived so cruelly in the past wouldn't forgive so easily, even if a wrong had been levied unintentionally.

"I'm sorry." It was all she could think to say. "I didn't mean to mislead you in any way."

He inclined his head and studied her for a moment that stretched out like an eternity. "You had no idea who you were until just a few hours ago. There's no reason to apologize."

"I know, but…" She drew a deep breath for courage. "I know how much truth means to you."

A ghost of a smile haunted his lips. "You remember that conversation, do you?"

Her own lips twitched with the need to return that smile. "I remember all our conversations."

"Tea? Or did you remember that you like coffee, after all?" He sounded weary, but he still managed a teasing tone.

"Tea. Always tea or cocoa."

"It'll be dark out for a while now. We should prepare for what the next few hours may bring."

He was right. Only she didn't intend to wait for the enemy to act. She intended to be the one acting, not reacting. She couldn't bring down all of them, but if she got *him* the organization would fall apart.

"We need to talk," she told him.

"So talk." He moved toward the kitchen even as he urged her to say what was on her mind.

"There are a lot of blank spots in my memory," she admitted as she leaned against the counter and watched him put the kettle on the stove.

"Since we don't know the method used to corrupt your memory, that could change in time."

"The last thing I recall before waking up on that gurney is being strapped to a table with an intravenous line running into a vein." She pushed her hair behind her ears. "I don't know what they did to me after that, but whatever it was, it worked."

"Temporarily," O'Brien countered. "You're remembering more with each passing hour, I would suspect."

He was right. She recalled more now than she had only a few minutes ago, when she had awakened. She looked out at the lake. The moon hung low over the water, glimmering in the darkness.

"I remember that when no one else believed in me, you did."

He hadn't shaved. The dark stubble on his face lent a rugged appeal. She doubted he let that side show often. She liked it.

He plopped a teabag into a mug. "Don't forget, that's my job."

True, but she sensed there was more to it than that. "I think you needed someone to save, and I was it." That hadn't exactly come out the way she'd intended. "I mean—"

"I know what you mean."

"No. I don't think you do." She put her hand on his arm when he would have reached to pour himself another cup of coffee. "You're way out of your comfort zone. You went there for me. I appreciate it more than you can know."

He moved away from her touch and poured his coffee. She shouldn't be surprised. This was a professional relationship, nothing personal. Even if some moments had felt entirely personal.

"What can you tell me about the element who wants you erased?"

*Erased.* That was a perfect description of what they wanted. She had gotten in the way, thrown a wrench into their plans, and now they wanted to expunge her.

"Highly intelligent." She considered the murky facts filed away in her memory so haphazardly. She wondered if her head would ever really be on straight again. "Cunning. They know what they're doing. The main thrust of the organization is here in Chicago. There are branches in New York and D.C., but communication central is here." That had been her target. Infiltrate at the management level. Get the *him* whose identity remained unknown to her.

"Do you recall names or locations?" He poured boiling water into her mug.

"Some. But nothing important." She added the sugar and stirred. "What we need is the top man."

"Have you met the chief?"

She nodded. "He's the guy who showed up at the coffee shop. He calls himself Chet Wheeler, but the real Chet Wheeler is dead." Angela had to look away from O'Brien's discerning eyes. She didn't like to think about Wheeler.

"You feel responsible for his death."

Ah, the shrink was coming out. "Yeah." She met his gaze. "I do. Maybe because he took a bullet for me early in this operation. I made a mistake and he died because of it." She'd had to pretend she didn't even know him. Had watched those thugs dump his body. Her stomach churned violently. Somehow the drugs had scrambled her memory and she had considered herself Wheeler's killer. God only knew what else she'd confused.

"You know he did what he was trained to do, just as you would have or may have to someday."

"Yeah, yeah." She searched O'Brien's eyes. "Don't analyze me, Doc. I know the deal, I just don't like it."

"Is this tough persona the real Angela Tapley? Or was Sande Williams the real you that hides behind the title 'special agent'?"

"If you're trying to get on my good side, it's not working." She sipped her tea. "Look." She exhaled a breath of frustration. "I know you're accustomed to doing things your way, but I have to warn you, I have a plan, and I won't be dissuaded from carrying it out."

He schooled his expression, denying her access to what he was feeling. "Let's hear this plan of yours."

"Since I can't tell you who or where the bad guys are, I have no choice but to attempt to lure them into the open. Otherwise," she interjected quickly, when he would have protested, "we might never get the people responsible for Windy's death. Or any of the others'."

"You need to know that I won't allow you to risk your life to accomplish your goal. My job is to protect you, while attempting to solve this case."

She got the picture. "So you, as a representative of the Colby Agency, feel compelled to ensure my safety, since I'm your client."

"That's correct." He knocked back a slug of coffee. "I have an obligation to ensure your safety twenty-four–seven until this is done."

"Great." She set her tea aside. "That's an easy fix. You're fired."

# *Chapter Fifteen*

Patrick called in reinforcements.

Ian Michaels and Simon Ruhl, along with Lucas Camp, Victoria's husband, were on hand to help persuade Angela to see reason.

She sat on the sofa, arms crossed over her chest, one jean-clad leg over the other. So far she refused to be swayed.

Patrick shook his head. "You're not thinking this through. What good is luring out this man who calls himself Agent Wheeler if you can't take him down?"

Those blue eyes that, on Sande, had been so soft and vulnerable turned to rock-hard ice as he watched. "What makes you think I can't take him down on my own?"

Ian Michaels flashed Patrick a glance that said *touché*. Not funny.

"History," Patrick responded. "You weren't able

to take him down before. There's no logical reason to believe that has changed."

Those icy-blue eyes glittered with fury. "Keep in mind that the last time Wheeler and I met, I was mentally incapacitated."

"That's an excuse," Patrick countered. "You can either do the job or you can't." Now he'd really pissed her off. Even he realized that had been a cheap shot, but he'd passed the point of desperation about an hour ago. He had to make her see reason.

Angela leaped to her feet, the movement rapid and fluid. She didn't even move the way Sande had. The memory of Patrick's wife's two personas crashed into his mind. He booted it back to that area of gray matter he rarely accessed. Angela's situation was not the same. The Sande persona had not arisen of her own free will.

"If I don't stop him, he'll just keep extending the network of his organization. He's like a virus and he's out of control. When this operation started, there was one group here in Chicago. Then he moved into D.C. and then New York. He won't stop until someone stops him." She strolled right up to Patrick and stood toe to toe. "He won't leave his protective cocoon for any reason other than to eradicate his one mistake. Me."

Patrick refused to back down. He met that glacial

glare with fire in his own. "That's exactly why I can't let you do that."

"She has a point."

Patrick whipped his gaze to the man who'd spoken. Lucas Camp. Most of the spy world referred to him as the Legend. Right now he was a pain in Patrick's neck. "What?"

"Lucas is right." Ian pushed away from the back of the sofa. He'd been perched there since he arrived, enjoying the sparring between Patrick and Angela far too much. "She's the one loose end Wheeler would surface to personally take care of. His operation has been far too perfectly executed until now. He can't risk her continued survival."

Patrick threw his hands up. "It would be helpful if you didn't encourage her."

Using his cane, Lucas levered himself from his chair. He took a couple of steps in Patrick's direction. "The man who refers to himself as Wheeler is the one we must stop in order to close down this organization he's built. As Angela pointed out, he's not going to take the risk of being trapped without one hell of a reason. She might very well be the only motivation compelling enough to get the job done."

When Patrick would have argued, Simon stepped into the conversation. "I'm sure Lucas is not suggesting that Angela conduct this kind of sting alone.

She'll need backup and we'll need a flawless plan. As a team we can accomplish both goals—taking down Wheeler and protecting her."

Angela started to protest, but Lucas cut her off with a stern glance. "No negotiations, madam. This is the way we do things."

Patrick couldn't imagine anyone in his or her right mind arguing with that directive.

"All right. If that's the way it's got to be." She looked from one implacable face to the next. "How are we going to do this?"

Angela was still a little behind the curve. Her cognitive reactions were way too slow. Otherwise there was no way these guys would have bested her. But she could work with this. It wasn't like she had a choice.

At least not on this side of the starting line. When she got in the race she would do things her way.

"Our first move should be to contact Wheeler," Ian suggested.

"It will be difficult to formulate a plan of action until contact has been made," Simon agreed. "We need to see how this guy is going to want to play the game."

Exactly. Angela would have recognized the logic and strategic skills of a fellow agent even if O'Brien hadn't already informed her that Simon Ruhl was former FBI. He fit the profile of a special agent.

"The plan is simple," she announced, determined

to run this show in spite of the massive quantity of testosterone permeating the room. "I give Wheeler a call and let him know I'm ready to come in. I pretend that to my knowledge, now that my memory is back, the whole Sande Williams persona never happened."

"You think it's going to be that simple?" O'Brien demanded. "Wheeler wouldn't have gotten this far if he were stupid."

"I know what I'm about." She was sick of everyone telling her what she should do. It was past time to get this party started. "I'd like to make the call now, please."

Ian Michaels placed his cell phone on the coffee table and attached a small accessory. When he turned it on she recognized it for what it was. A call diverter.

"When you make the call it will appear that it's coming from wherever you choose."

"The coffee shop on Broadway," she said promptly. Wheeler had shown up there when they were supposed to meet Lyons, which was likely his not so subtle way of letting her know he was responsible for the detective's demise. Wheeler had likely suspected that Lyons was onto him. Poor detective. He hadn't had a chance against such a slick piece of work.

Simon made a call to the office and got the number for the coffee shop. Once it was entered into the diverter, she was set. All she had to do was place the call.

"Can we have a moment?" O'Brien asked, his gaze pinning her with a "yes, I mean you" glare.

"Sure."

She followed him to the study down the hall. The door was hardly closed when he wheeled on her. "You need to lose the attitude."

"What attitude?" She set her hands on her hips and gave him the same hard-core glower he aimed in her direction. "What you see is what you get."

He shook his head slowly. "You might want the others to believe that you're a completely different person from the woman we knew as Sande Williams. But I know better. Beneath that overconfident exterior is that same scared-as-hell individual who's confused and uncertain about herself and her future."

Doubt closed her throat. "You're wrong. I know exactly who I am and what I'm doing. I'm up to this. Are you?"

He ignored her question. "I didn't get you this far only to see you take a suicide plunge now." His nostrils flared with the anger simmering beneath that oh-so-controlled surface.

It wasn't the time, but she couldn't help wondering if the Doc ever lost control.

Probably not.

"What's wrong? You never took a chance before? Is playing it safe the way you like to go through life?

If so, you're missing out on all the fun. Chill out and let's get this done."

Fury tightening his lips, he clasped her shoulders in those big hands and gave her a little shake.

"Wow. Finally, a gut reaction!" she exclaimed.

And then he kissed her. Maybe just to shut her up, but the effect was the same. She melted against him like ice cream dropped on a hot sidewalk. His lips were desperate, as if he hadn't kissed in a really long time. His body trembled with the fury she'd seen in his eyes.

She snaked her arms around his neck and leaned into the kiss…into that muscular chest. It felt good. It felt damn good.

Then he stopped. Drew back just enough to catch his breath.

"That shouldn't have happened."

She rose on tiptoe and kissed his damp lips again. "No, but I'm glad it did."

Before he could gather his wits, she dropped her arms, darted around him and returned to where the rest of the crew waited.

Time to make this thing happen. If she got it going now she wouldn't have to worry about O'Brien coming up with any more logical reasons she shouldn't. He was way too rattled.

"Let's make that call," she announced as she joined the others.

"Keep in mind," Lucas recommended, "he's going to want to meet with you as soon as possible to finish the cleanup of this mess. Don't let him push you into cutting yourself short on time."

Angela nodded. O'Brien had nailed her with his psychoanalyzing. She'd pushed the edge of cockiness to get their attention and her way. But inside, where no one but he could see, she was terrified. Maybe it had taken him pointing it out for her to acknowledge it. Bad timing.

She gritted her teeth against the emotion. No amount of fear was going to stop her from taking this bastard down.

She picked up the phone and entered the number she somehow knew by heart. Just as instinctively, her heart started a ferocious pounding.

The voice she would recognize on any side of hell answered on the second ring.

"This is Tapley. I need to come in."

There was a pause.

Her pulse reacted.

He named a place and time.

The determination and attitude that had earned her the top spot in her Bureau training class roared through her. "That won't work for me," she retorted without missing a beat. "Mercy General's morgue, two o'clock."

She pushed the end call button and handed the phone back to Ian. "Good job," he offered.

What the hell had made her pick that location?

Maybe because that was where this damned game had left off.

Maybe because she hadn't been thinking beyond her need for vengeance.

Truth was, she was worried.

But that wasn't going to stop her.

"We have three hours," Simon announced. "Let's lay out a strategy."

"Detective Cates should be included," O'Brien advised.

Angela wasn't so sure how she felt about the detective. Lyons had given her mixed signals, at least what she had seen of him before she'd sunk into the Sande Williams persona. She'd met with him twice before her brain got scrambled. Cates was an unknown factor. Lyons had never mentioned him and neither had Wheeler. Maybe that was a good thing.

"Call him," Angela agreed, surprising O'Brien. "It couldn't hurt."

Her plan wouldn't include any of them, anyway. She might as well play nice until the moment she needed to make the leap into a solo act.

Barely half an hour later the detective joined them at the Colby Agency safe house. Shane Allen, another of O'Brien's associates, had arrived with several duffel bags of equipment and protective gear.

When the detective had been brought up to speed, he sat back a moment and considered Angela. She met his scrutiny without a blink. He could trust her or not. Didn't really make a difference to her.

"You sure don't seem like the same lady I met yesterday," he commented.

"I'll take that as a compliment, Detective," she replied just as dryly.

"Two hours from now," Simon interjected, getting down to business, "we move into place at the hospital."

Simon and Ian spent the next few minutes outlining their strategy for trapping Wheeler in the hospital's basement. All of which had to be accomplished without alerting security before the takedown. There was no way to know who at the hospital was working with Wheeler, but someone must be, considering they had denied Sande had ever been in their facility.

"You'll be fully wired," O'Brien said to Angela. "Simon and Ian will be aware of every sound and movement around you."

She had a bad feeling about him leaving his name out of that scenario. "And where will you be?"

"I'll be right next to you."

No way. She waved her hands in denial. "That

won't work. No one can be in the room. Wheeler won't show if there's a warm body anywhere near there, besides mine. He'll use thermal imaging." She looked from one man to the other. "I'm telling you he won't take any chances."

"He'll never know I'm there even if he does use thermal imaging," O'Brien challenged. "Trust me."

"He's too smart to be fooled by any of your twelfth-hour theatrics." Didn't O'Brien understand? If he got too close they'd both end up dead.

"You do your part," O'Brien insisted, "the rest of us will do ours."

Angela turned to Lucas Camp for backup, but that wasn't happening. All the men in the room were determined to protect her. She'd spent a lifetime proving she could take care of herself in a man's world. This was not the time to take a major step back.

"Let's get prepped." Ian stood. "We'll need to test the communications."

O'Brien pulled her aside to speak privately again as the others gathered around the gear. One look into his dark eyes and she knew he was not buying her team act for a second.

"Whatever you've got up your sleeve, Angela," he warned, "you'd better think twice. I'm not letting you out of my sight."

She smiled, wishing it wasn't genuine. There was

just something about him that got to her, way beneath the skin. Miles deeper than anyone else had ever gotten. "You think you know me, O'Brien, but you don't. If I decide to make an unplanned move, you won't see it coming in time to react."

He held her gaze for three, four, five seconds. The kaleidoscope of emotions there took her breath away.

"That's what scares me," he murmured. "That I won't see it coming until it's too late."

As long as it saved his life, she wasn't worried.

# Chapter Sixteen

Mercy General's morgue was in the basement.

Getting five men into place in authorized-personnel-only territory wasn't a simple task.

Patrick tucked the final video chip onto Angela's jacket. The Colby Agency generally coordinated operations with the security team of any facility they were forced to utilize, but this situation was different.

They couldn't risk involving anyone on staff at the hospital, since the administration had staunchly denied any knowledge of Sande Williams having been in their facility in any capacity.

"You should get into position with Ian and Simon," Angela told Patrick, her patience obviously growing thin. Ian and Simon were just inside the walk-in cooler, on the other side of the massive door across the room. It was close and the chilly temperature would prevent their body heat from showing up on a thermal scan.

"There's time," Patrick said, blowing her off.

"Everyone else is in place," she nagged.

Patrick had a very bad feeling about all of this. Lucas and Cates were in the lobby directly above their position. They were watching and listening via the communications links placed on Angela, as well as positioned around the room where she would confront Wheeler.

And still Patrick couldn't get the idea out of his head that things weren't going to go down as planned. Angela had some sort of scheme up her sleeve. He sensed it with every cell in his body.

He donned the lab coat with its borrowed badge, along with the standard black-framed eyeglasses, and laid facedown on the floor. He would be playing the part of the morgue attendant Wheeler was supposed to believe Angela had disabled. The actual morgue attendant had been persuaded to have coffee in the cafeteria with the Colby Agency receptionist. This operation had a thirty-minute window. It was going to be close.

Five minutes and Wheeler was supposed to show. Simon, Ian and Lucas had already discussed with Patrick the idea that Wheeler surely wouldn't get himself hemmed into a situation like this.

Angela's response to Wheeler when she made the call had to have been a code of some sort for a different location. As Patrick had pointed out to her before, Wheeler hadn't gotten to the top of the scumbag chain by being stupid.

Patrick counted off the seconds. Any minute now he was certain Angela would do the unexpected.

The thought had no more formed in his brain than she did exactly that. She shoved the pin dangling from a chain on the handle into the walk-in cooler door, locking Simon and Ian inside, and made a run for the corridor.

"Damn it!" Patrick scrambled to his feet and rushed after her.

ANGELA HAD TO HURRY. She reached the stairwell door, opened it wide and let go. Instead of hitting the stairs, she slipped into the same janitor's closet she'd used the last time she was here.

She held her breath. Ignored the voices shouting in her ear via the communications link. Simon and Ian were pissed.

O'Brien's pounding footsteps passed the janitor's closet and headed up the stairs. He'd likely seen the stairwell door as it closed leading him to reason that she'd taken the stairs.

She had to work fast now. One by one she stripped off the audio and visual communications links. Then she ran for the elevator.

Lucas or Cates would rush down to free Simon and Ian. One or the other would have hit the elevator call button by now.

As if she'd coordinated her efforts with all involved the elevator dinged, announcing its arrival. She hid around the corner and waited for Lucas to make his way toward the morgue. Just before the doors glided closed, she bolted for the elevator. She hit the lobby button and a few seconds later she was there.

Using the parking garage exit, she was out of the building and putting through a call to Wheeler within two minutes of their original meeting time.

"South side of Mercy General," she told the bastard. "Now."

That was the strategy she and Wheeler had always used. The first meeting place stated was never the one. A secondary location was always given, to ensure a way out of exactly the scenario she'd left behind in the morgue.

Another of those stabs of guilt landed deep in her gut. O'Brien would never forgive her for deceiving him. But this was the way it had to be. Wheeler would never have rendezvoused with her unless she was completely alone. He damn sure wouldn't do it in an area where he might be cornered. Like the morgue. That had been a ruse in order to better control the actions of O'Brien and his associates.

She knew how Wheeler operated.

This was the only way.

He had to go down.

The only way to really stop him was to kill him. That was her plan. She might die in the process but it would be worth it if she got him.

Angela stopped at the corner of the building to catch her breath and look for Wheeler's car.

Before she killed him she would like to know one thing. What had he done to muddy her memory?

Maybe she would never know.

Wouldn't matter, anyway. She'd likely be dead.

A hand closed over her mouth at the same time a strong arm coiled around her chest and jerked her up against a hard body.

"Don't move. Don't make a sound."

She fought his hold, twisted her head to confirm what her ears heard.

O'Brien.

Damn! He was going to ruin everything.

She struggled against his grasp.

"I'm going to take my hand off your mouth. Scream or run and I swear I'll pin you to the ground."

"He's coming," she snarled as soon as his fingers loosened on her lips. "If he sees you he'll disappear and this chance will be lost forever."

"You think I don't know that?" The ferocity in

O'Brien's eyes cut straight through her. "We'll do this the right way."

The blood roared in her ears in time with the pounding in her chest.

"What's your plan?" she demanded, ready to howl with frustration.

"See that building across the street?"

She looked past the cars moving slowly along the asphalt to the four-story medical equipment and supplies shop. "Yeah, so what?"

"Simon is taking a position there."

That was impossible. She'd locked Simon and Ian in the cooler, and they had no idea where she was. O'Brien had gotten lucky when he took the south side looking for her.

"To your right," he murmured against her forehead, his lips distracting her, even as furious as she was at the moment, "Ian is watching from that clinic. Shane is in the parking garage watching from the second level."

"That's impossible," she argued, giving voice to her thoughts. "They couldn't have known which way I would go."

O'Brien laughed. "I told you I was onto your strategy. I added an extra audio link you didn't know about." He plucked it from her hair. "We heard what you told Wheeler."

Pride welled right alongside the fury and frustration. "You caught me," she confessed. "Now what's your plan? We've got one shot. Make it count."

"I intend to."

Before she could analyze the certainty in his tone, O'Brien set her aside and dashed toward the street.

"No!"

The one word she'd managed to utter echoed between the buildings as if heralding Wheeler's arrival. She watched, the action seem to happen in slow motion, as his sedan rolled along the now deserted stretch of asphalt.

She started after O'Brien, but powerful hands grabbed and restrained her.

"Take it easy, Tapley. We've got the situation under control."

She twisted around as best she could to look Lucas Camp in the eye. "Wheeler will kill him."

Lucas smiled. "Not today."

Her attention swung back to the street, where Wheeler was attempting to squeal away. A police cruiser skidded to a stop in the street, blocking his path. Detective Cates jumped from the passenger side and leveled a bead on Wheeler's sedan.

Wheeler rammed into Reverse and barreled in the other direction. This time two cruisers blocked his escape route. At the same time, Simon Ruhl, Ian

Michaels and Shane Allen approached from different directions, each with a weapon trained on the driver of the sedan.

Wheeler was trapped.

Angela shook her head. "Unbelievable."

"That's the Colby Agency."

She hadn't realized she'd said the words aloud until Lucas responded.

But he was right.

The Colby Agency was unstoppable.

Unbelievable.

## Chapter Seventeen

Angela watched through the two-way mirror in the observation booth as Kale Harkey, aka Special Agent Chet Wheeler, spilled his guts in an interview room. He had cut a deal with the district attorney to avoid the death penalty. He'd personally executed more than a dozen people in four different states. But the information he possessed was more valuable than the good feeling everyone in this booth would get from watching him take his final breath.

The identity theft operation was secondary to the mole operation he had going on. The list of corporations and research facilities he had infiltrated, including the hospital where Angela had awakened, was staggering. The look-alikes he'd ferreted out and hired had all possessed the precise skills he'd needed. Not one had known his or her fate once Harkey had finished with them. He would have a long, long time in prison to think about his many sins.

He'd admitted to using on Angela an experimental drug that corrupted memory. None of his other guinea pigs had lived long enough to evaluate the long-term effects of the drug. The dream she'd had about a man ordering her termination and a woman arguing against it had been real, to some degree. The woman, the murdered Nancy Childers in whose house Angela had lived, Harkey's subordinate, had not wanted any part of murdering a federal agent. That hadn't stopped this jerk from using the drugs or murdering whomever he chose.

Angela was scheduled for testing later in the week to ensure she had no permanent damage. The research facility Harkey had stolen the drug from was more than willing to conduct the testing. She was the first human test subject and they were anxious to see the results.

The director of the FBI had called to congratulate Angela. He'd even offered her a position at Quantico. She hadn't decided just yet if she was taking it. Maybe.

"Well, Agent Tapley," Detective Cates said as Wheeler wound up his confession, "I have to say, you nailed that bastard but good." They had learned that Detective Lyons had planned to turn over the missing documents from his case file to O'Brien, but Harkey had gotten to him first.

Angela smiled. "Of course. That's what special agents do." She shook the detective's hand.

"Don't be a stranger," he called after her as she left the booth.

She'd heard and seen enough. She was out of here.

The door burst open behind her before she could escape to the elevator.

"Did you really think you were going to get away without a proper goodbye?"

She hesitated before turning to face O'Brien. She'd wanted to skip this part. But that wasn't happening now.

"Goodbyes are overrated, Doc."

He was all spit and polished today. Back to the old Patrick O'Brien before she'd barged into his life. Navy suit with matching tie, white shirt. Very crisp. Damn handsome.

He moved in toe to toe with her. "You know, I don't let anyone address me that way anymore."

One corner of her mouth lifted in a wry smile. "You'll get over it."

That sweet, fragile Sande Williams whom O'Brien had gotten a glimpse of had finally fully morphed back into the badass special agent she'd always been beneath that vulnerable drug-induced facade. She hoped not to ever go there again. She was no shrinking violet.

"I'll keep that in mind, Agent."

"I guess I'll see you around." She didn't have to be back in D.C. until next week after the testing. A few days of R & R would come in handy. She was tired. Mostly she just wanted to relax and recharge. She hit the call button for the elevator.

"You headed back to D.C. right away?" he asked, before those damn elevator doors could open, letting her escape.

They hadn't discussed her plans. Primarily because it was too hard. Yeah, yeah, it was dumb. But she'd developed some silly attachment to the Doc. She'd hoped to avoid the whole thing by slipping away unnoticed. Now that was blown all to hell.

"Not for a few days," she admitted, her attention fixed on those unmoving doors. *Hurry!*

"I see."

No he didn't.

He would wonder why she'd opted to stay in town, but hadn't mentioned it to him.

Damn it.

She couldn't have him thinking there were hard feelings, or something crazy like that.

"I…" She shrugged. "I just need time to think."

He inclined his head. "About?"

Well, hell, there was no hiding anything from this guy. "About us." If that blasted elevator didn't hurry up…

"Us?" He nodded. "I see."

There he went again. "No, you don't see."

"Sure. I get it. You're not interested in strings or attachments."

Did he have a crystal ball or what?

"This has just been a little fast and awkward because of the drugs." Okay, that was a lie. She didn't have a lot of experience in this territory. The way she'd lied to him about the meet with Wheeler, she was actually surprised he even wanted to speak to her again. "Truth is, I don't really do relationships."

"I don't, either," he admitted. "Especially with a woman who doesn't think twice about avoiding the truth. As you know, I have issues."

She rolled her eyes. "I did what I had to do."

"And so did I," he retorted.

"So." She shrugged. "Maybe we both learned something."

"Maybe there's a lot more to learn."

She stared right into those dark eyes, bared her soul for the first time in a really, really long time. "Seriously, I don't do very well with relationships. I'm my own woman. I'm a type A personality. I don't like anything getting in the way of my work. I guess I'm a workaholic. I rarely sleep. I hate pets. I'm a slob. I can't cook. Basically, I'm—"

He kissed her. Once again probably to shut her up.

But it didn't matter. Because when their lips met the rest of the world dissolved into nothingness. He was all that mattered. Him and the way he kissed her. She couldn't get enough. Her arms flew around his neck and she kissed him back with all she had.

She ignored the ding of the elevator arriving. Who cared? Right now all she wanted to do was kiss this man.

When she had to breathe, she pulled back just enough to catch her breath. "I love the way you kiss me." What a lame thing to confess!

"I love kissing you," he murmured against her lips.

He kissed her nose, her forehead, then settled his gaze on hers. "You can't go until we see what this thing between us is all about. This could be real."

*Real.* Definitely. She smiled. "Then I guess we're going to your place."

Dr. Patrick O'Brien took her hand and led the way. For the first time in her life she kind of liked someone else taking charge.

She could get used to him.

Maybe she already had.

# Chapter Eighteen

Victoria Colby-Camp reviewed the final reports on the Sande Williams case. She shook her head. It was such a shame that people disappeared so frequently and were never found. Their identities stolen and used until no longer needed, then discarded like so much trash.

Something had to be done to stop this travesty.

Victoria thought of her son, Jim, and how he'd been stolen away from her. Nothing the police had done—nothing she had done—had worked. The whole process had been like looking for a needle in a haystack during a windstorm. Sadly, even the Bureau's elite units often couldn't find the missing or stop the theft of a person's most personal asset—his or her identity. Too much red tape. Too many rules and regulations.

The Colby Agency needed to do its part and more.

The thought of one of her beloved grandchildren going missing was more than Victoria could bear.

She had to take steps to ensure the Colby name continued to be synonymous with premier private investigations.

Inspiration sent a smile sliding across her lips. Oh, yes. There was more she could do. A lot more.

Victoria buzzed Mildred and requested that Ian and Simon join her. The answer was so simple, Victoria couldn't believe she hadn't considered it before. The Colby Agency would institute a new department. A reconnaissance group focused exclusively on finding the lost.

When her top staff members had joined her, Victoria announced her plan.

"Excellent idea," Simon declared. "This would take our retrieval efforts to the next level."

"Agreed," Ian seconded. "We should consider bringing Angela Tapley on board for this group. She would be a great asset."

"That's a marvelous suggestion." Victoria was extremely pleased. She had always prided herself on doing all she could to help parents find their missing children. But this could go a step beyond even that.

Whoever was missing, wherever they were last seen, the Colby Agency would find them and bring them home. No matter how long it took. Unlike the cases the police often had to set aside, the Colby Agency would never give up.

"This," Simon commented, "is the kind of effort that keeps the Colby Agency one step ahead of the rest."

That was Victoria's single goal when it came to the agency. To ensure that it was the best in the business. Her goal could only be accomplished one way: never stop evolving and growing. It was absolutely essential in order to keep up with the changing world.

She turned to the window and looked out over the city she loved.

This latest case had been particularly hard. The Colby Agency had lost one of its own. As painful as that reality was, Victoria refused to be defeated. She would keep moving forward.

This was yet another new beginning.

\* \* \* \* \*

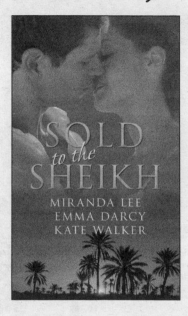

# FREE!

## 2 Books
### and a surprise gift!

We would like to take this opportunity to thank you for reading this Mills & Boon® book by offering you the chance to take TWO more specially selected titles from the Intrigue series absolutely FREE! We're also making this offer to introduce you to the benefits of the Mills & Boon® Book Club™—

- ★ **FREE home delivery**
- ★ **FREE gifts and competitions**
- ★ **FREE monthly Newsletter**
- ★ **Exclusive Mills & Boon Book Club offers**
- ★ **Books available before they're in the shops**

Accepting these FREE books and gift places you under no obligation to buy, you may cancel at any time, even after receiving your free shipment. Simply complete your details below and return the entire page to the address below. You don't even need a stamp!

**YES!** Please send me 2 free Intrigue books and a surprise gift. I understand that unless you hear from me, I will receive 4 superb new titles every month for just £3.19 each, postage and packing free. I am under no obligation to purchase any books and may cancel my subscription at any time. The free books and gift will be mine to keep in any case.

19ZEF

Ms/Mrs/Miss/Mr ............................................Initials ............................

**BLOCK CAPITALS PLEASE**

Surname ..................................................................................................

Address ..................................................................................................

.................................................................................................................

.................................................................Postcode ..............................

**Send this whole page to:**
**UK: FREEPOST CN81, Croydon, CR9 3WZ**